The Ballad of Robin and King Richard

Table of Contents

Content Warning:

This book contains a lot of sensitive topics, including but not limited to:

Homophobia, biphobia, transphobia, and gender dysphoria

Infertility

Child abuse (emotional, mentions of physical and CSA)

Emotional abuse and domestic violence

Mentions of drug abuse

Religious trauma

Eating disorder/negative body image

Gun violence/death

Death of a parent

Explicit and offensive language

For a more thorough description, check out

arturfaye.com/triggerwarnings

Reader discretion is advised.

ISBN: 979-8-9872712-3-0 (ebook) | 979-8-9872712-4-7 (paperback)

To the queer youth of the past, the present, and the future

To our brothers and sisters and siblings that we have lost

To our queer elders who have gone through so much hardship and are
still standing

To our siblings that dealt with struggles yesterday, today, and tomorrow

The Ballad of Robin and King Richard

Prologue

Laying next to my wife in our bed, she starts to doze off. I can't fall asleep, though. I'm too excited. To think that in a few days I'm going to be a father. I know I've had quite a while to process it all, but it still seems so impossible. I just can't comprehend the fact we're gonna have a little baby girl.

I can't wait to hold her, and spoil her. I want her to know she is loved to the moon and back. That I care about her and only want what's best for her. She's gonna be such a lucky kid.

My number one priority is to make sure she's happy and healthy. I don't want her to have to grow up too fast or see things that she shouldn't yet see. I want her to be a kid and have a childhood. And I'm gonna do everything I can to make sure of it. She deserves the world.

"Dick? Are you even going to try to fall asleep?"

I can't help but smile. "No."

It makes my wife laugh. "You need to sleep. Once the baby's born and comes home, you're not going to get any."

"I know, but I can't help it." I can't wait for the moment my little baby is born and I get to have her in my arms. To see her with my own eyes and be with her.

It's gonna be so beautiful.

"Well, at least try. For both our sakes." Carol turns over to look at me and beams. She looks so amazing, even if she's just lying in bed next to me in her maternity pajamas. In the darkness, her blonde hair and smile light up the whole world.

"You're so pretty," I tell her. I've been making sure to let her know more how beautiful she is. Recently, she's been very negative of herself, especially about her body. It's rough for her, so every time I think to myself how beautiful or pretty or hot she is, I make sure she knows.

"You always say that."

"And I always mean it." I grin at her. "I love you."

"I love you, too." She gives me a kiss. "Now come over here and sleep."

"I'll try." I scoot over to my wife and put my arms around her as she slowly falls asleep. I really try to doze off, but I just end up staying awake most of the night. It's fine though, because it just gives me more time to cherish my wife and our baby.

Chapter 1

Robin

ou won't get away with this, Sheriff of Nottingham!" I cry out loud enough for him to hear. I can tell it works when he stops in his tracks and turns to face me.

"Oh really? Well then, I challenge you to a duel."

"A duel to the death!"

"Then a duel to the death it shall be." He brings out his sword as he bends his knees, getting in his stance to start the fight. I pull out my own from my scabbard, smirking a bit. This battle is going to be so easy. I know his every weak point.

He holds his sword out, waiting for me to hold mine against his, which would signal the beginning of our duel. With no hesitation—and I make sure of it—I put my weapon against his own.

Our fight begins.

He strikes hard and fast, swinging the blade around. The first few hits I block with ease. As I block and parry, I notice his swings slowly start getting far from me. There's no point even trying on my end. His inexperience really shows. It bothers me because I know why he's doing it, and I don't want to go to bed. "Dad, come on. Take it seriously!"

"I am taking it seriously."

"No, you're not. You're just phoning it in because Mom said it's almost time for bed."

Dad sighs, his face falling a bit. I don't think he was expecting me to catch on to it. I don't know why he thinks that because I'm not stupid. I'm not a little kid anymore; I'm almost old enough to go to middle school, and little kids don't go to middle school. "Sorry, kiddo. I'll take it seriously this time. Promise."

"Thank you," I say to him. It makes Dad smile. "Now, Sheriff, let us duel to the death!"

With that, we both bring our swords back up, and this time Dad isn't cheesing it. Our wooden weapons collide, and he immediately goes for the attack. I dodge out of the way, just in the nick of time, and while Dad is off his footing, I attack back. As I do, he almost gets hit, but barely stumbles out of the way in time. I start to sweat a bit with how fast it's going. It's nothing compared to Dad, though. He's nothing but sweat.

I just have to find my entrance for the stab. As I swing my sword at him, I search for any and every opportunity. It becomes very evident that he leaves himself quite open when he blocks. He tries to slash me, but I avoid it and go for my own attack. I make sure to do so a little slower than usual (to throw him off a bit), and go as quick as I can for the stab.

"No! I've been defeated!" Dad groans. As he falls to the ground, he has his final dramatic cries, but he grabs me and takes me down with him. I can't help but smile and laugh as my dad hugs me and pulls me down. He never wants to go down alone and helpless; he wants to go down fighting. And right when I'm at my weakest, he starts tickling my armpits.

"Dad! Dad!" I try to tell him to quit it, but I can only giggle. "Dad! Stop!"

"Oh, fine," he whines, but he lets go of me. My father sighs as he looks up at the sky. I look up as well, finding the stars up above us. It's so nice to see them so big and bright. Soon enough we're going to have to go to the city, where the stars aren't as shiny and magical. I hate how they lose their sparkle, and I don't understand why. My cousins think stars are boring because of how dull they look, and it always bugs me. If they came out here and saw them in all their glory, then they would understand how amazing they are.

Then again, maybe I just don't get why someone wouldn't want to live in the country. It's so nice out here, with trees and stars and the clean air. It's so refreshing. The city honestly makes me claustrophobic. I don't know how anyone can feel comfortable living there all the time.

"Hey, kiddo." Dad shakes me a bit to get my attention. "Remember what I taught you about the stars?"

"Yeah." Dad loves the stars. Well, anything about the outdoors. Even if he's said something about a certain tree a hundred times, he always gets excited as if it's the first. Mom finds it annoying after the second time, but it makes me smile. Seeing him happy makes me happy.

"Which constellation is that one?" He points to a collection of stars that, strung together, kinda looks like a sideways "Y".

"That's Taurus. Also known as Taurus the bull."

"Good job. And what's that one?" I can see Dad's smile creeping on his face as the next constellation he motions to looks like a man drawn by a preschooler.

"That's Perseus, duh!" I can't believe Dad would think I'd forget that one. One of my favorite characters is named after Perseus. Well, next to Robin Hood.

"Alright. Alright. No need to be a pepper in the snow. What about that one?"

This time, it looks like a pot with a handle. I remember Dad showing it to me before, but I can't remember what it's called. "What is it again?"

"That one is Ursa Minor, also known as the Little Dipper. And that star right there"—he points to the end of the handle—"is called Polaris. It's more commonly known as the North Star because it's always north."

"How is it always north? Doesn't it move like the other stars?"

"Well," Dad begins. I can tell he's getting giddy just from me asking the question. "Polaris is right above the north pole, so when the Earth is spinning, it's always in the same spot."

"But what about constellations and stars that you only see during certain months? The north star can't *always* be there."

"It is. And you want to know why?" Dad waits for a response, but only for a second before going on. He's too eager to tell me all that is bubbling inside him. "It's because the Earth is at a tilt."

"Yeah, that's why we have different seasons."

"Yes! And because of the tilt, that's why the position of the stars change, but as I said, Polaris is right above the north pole." Dad brings one of his arms at a tilt, as if it's the Earth on its axis, and with his other hand, he makes a fist following the line he made with his arm. "So when the Earth goes around the sun, or revolves around it"—he does his best to make his arm move in a circle, even though it's not possible—"it's always above us, and those of us in the northern hemisphere, where we are, can always see it. Pretty cool, huh?"

"Very cool," I say, partially because I want to make my dad beam. I know he likes teaching these things to me, and I'm glad he does. It's honestly very fascinating. It's so crazy that we live on a tilted sphere and don't fall off. I don't feel tilted, yet here I am on a tilted land. It just feels like it's flat, but it's not. That's insane.

"Gracie!" Mom's voice calls from inside the house. Just hearing my name makes me shiver. "Come on! It's time for bed."

"I don't wanna go to bed," I whine to Dad as he starts getting up, hoping that he can maybe let me stay out for just a little longer.

"We all need to go to bed. We got a busy day tomorrow, driving to the city."

"Why can't we stay here and everyone comes to us? They should come over here for once." I get up anyway. If Dad is agreeing with Mom, there's no point in arguing.

"Because everyone can fly into the city, but not everyone has a car to drive out to here. Besides, we don't have enough room for everybody."

I guess that's true.

"Now come on, let's get on to bed." Dad offers his hand, and I take it. The two of us walk to the back porch, where Mom's waiting. She gives me a frown. "Grace, why aren't you wearing your coat? I don't want you catching a cold, especially around Christmas."

"I don't like wearing my coat." It's too pink and frilly. It makes me feel... feel weird. I don't like it. Whatever feeling it is, it's worse when I wear a dress. Most days suck because I rarely get to wear anything but all the dresses Mom picks out.

"And I don't like it when you get sick. I want you to be healthy, you got that?" Mom moves a curl of my hair behind my ear. "I just want you to be fine and safe."

"I know."

Mom smiles. "Good." She gives me a big kiss on the forehead and ushers me up the stairs.

I get into my nightgown and brush my teeth while Mom straightens and braids my hair. It gets really hot when she straightens it, and we usually don't do it at night, but because we're leaving early tomorrow, she wants to get all the prep done before bed and braid it so it doesn't undo itself. My hair tends to do what it wants and curl every possible way.

With clean teeth and my straight hair in braids, it's time for bed. I hop under the pink covers, getting nice and warm.

"Now, remember," Mom begins, "we've got to get up early tomorrow to drive over to the city. And we're going to a different church for tomorrow, so make sure to be on your best behavior. And your cousins will be with you, so you'll have some friends."

"I know."

"Okay. Make sure to be up at five-thirty. Got it?"

"Got it."

"Alrighty. Goodnight. Love you." She gives me one more kiss and heads out of my room.

When Dad walks in, I know it's his turn. He comes over and tucks me in, tightening the sheets around me and making me feel cozy. "Did you know that people used the North Star to navigate around the world and figure out where they are?"

"Dick," I hear Mom groan from the door. We both know that means *leave her alone so she can go to bed.*

"Have a good night, kiddo. Sleep tight." He also gives me a kiss and starts heading for the door.

"Hey, Dad." I make sure to be loud enough so he can hear. He turns around. "Do you think Robin Hood used the North Star? Like to know where he was in England and where to go if he needed to go north?"

Dad thinks for a moment. "I think he would've used it. I mean, if he had to head north or south, it was very useful."

"Dick, she needs to go to sleep." Mom's very insistent on the amount of sleep I need.

"Alright. Night, Gracie." He blows me one more kiss and leaves my room with Mom.

Since I need to wake up early tomorrow, I turn off my light and get comfortable in my bed. Hopefully it's not too hectic in the morning. Everything should be packed, and hopefully Mom won't be a panicked mess (though she probably will. She always is when we leave for the city this time of year). Well, whatever happens will happen.

I close my eyes and try to drift off to sleep.

"Dick, I know you want to teach her things, but she's not five anymore. She's at the age where she's starting to become a woman. She needs to start focusing on more real and important things."

"The stars are important. And so is the outdoors."

"I mean, yes, but they're not things she needs to know. They're not things that are going to help her once she's an adult, like cooking, and how to sew, or the Bible for that matter! She's got to learn how to be a good godly woman, and playing Robin Hood isn't going to help with that."

"What's not good about Robin Hood?"

"Stealing. Stealing is not a good thing. That is a crime."

"Okay. Okay."

"At least start encouraging her to take her Bible studies more seriously, or that it can be fun to bake some desserts, or anything on how to be a contributing member of society."

"How can I do that?"

"She loves you, it's not that hard. I think also encouraging her to do more things with me would help. I know that you love her very much, but she's at that age where she needs to start being with more female figures. She needs a woman mentor to look up to. She's going to start going through things that, no offense, you aren't going to understand. I mean, she already is. She just needs a push in the right direction. It's only to help her."

Dad is quiet. "I guess you're right. I'll try pushing her in the right direction."

"Thank you. Now come on, let's get to bed."

Chapter 2

Robin

When we get to the church, Mom brings me to the bathroom and shoves me into a stall with all my clothes. She gives me a red dress with a big bow, a white cardigan, tights, and red shoes to match. I don't want to put it on, but at the same time, Mom's gonna be mad if I don't and make her late for service.

As I put my Sunday clothes on, I feel like something's creeping up on my skin, as if there are a bunch of hairy spiders climbing up on me with their eight legs devilishly stroking me and pinchers ready to bite. Chills start running up and down my body, and I swear I have goose-bumps even though it's pretty warm in the bathroom.

The feeling keeps picking at my skin, but I try to ignore it and zip up the dress as best I can in the back and throw the cardigan on. I also quickly get my tights and shoes on so I can exit the stall in hopes that maybe the spiders will disappear if I leave. I walk out—the creepy monsters still all over me—and to my mother, who is doing some makeup touch-ups in the mirror.

When she finishes her lashes, she puts her mascara away and turns to me. "Alrighty then. I'm going to just undo your braids real quick, okay?"

I nod.

My mom starts playing with my dirty blonde perfect hair, making sure the waves and curls of it are right and not all over the place or a mess. The ear and below is where the curls can show, as she always says. Thankfully, my roots are pretty straight, so it's not going to cause too many problems.

"I don't think I've seen y'all," a lady pipes up from the sink next to us. "My name's Emily. What are your names?"

"I'm Carol Wright, and this is my daughter, Grace." Mom's hand touches my shoulder as I do my best to have a cute grin. I know she's very proud of me and just wants to show me off. "We just drove in this morning. We're from a few hours south, but here to spend Christmas with the family."

"Oh! And who's that?"

"The Moores."

"Oh, the Moores! I know them, lovely people. James and Ruth?"

"Yes. They're my parents."

"Carol! Yes, I know you. They talk about you all the time! You're such a wonderful lady. If all your parents say is true, of course."

"Oh, it is." Mom's smile beams like God's holy light.

"And Grace, how old are you?" the lady asks me.

"Eleven."

"Well, let me tell you, sugar, you are a beautiful young lady, and that's a rare thing to come by."

Even though she's complimenting me, it's hard to keep up my smile. I don't really like being called beautiful, or a lady. I'd rather be called handsome, but no one has ever or will ever call me that.

"And you're so polite, too. You've done a wonderful job raising her."

"Oh, I've just brought her to church and made sure she reads her scriptures. She even annotates her Bible when she's doing her studies or listening to a sermon."

"Really? You got a smart girl on your hands."

"Don't even get me started on her report card." Mom chuckles. It's all A's. Everything just makes sense to me. I don't really struggle with much. On a test, I might miss a question or two, to which Mom always encourages me to do better, but I'm smart and a great kid, and Mom's very happy with having a charming, good-looking, intelligent kid like me. She tells me I'm perfect the way I am and that I'm her little angel and she loves me to the moon and back.

She's the greatest mom in the whole world.

"Well, you got quite the lucky little rabbit." The lady laughs. "Hopefully I'll see you guys after service. It's going to start soon, so I should probably let you two finish up. Tell James and Ruth I said hi."

"I will," Mom assures. With the lady now gone, Mom faces me in front of the mirror and finishes with my hair. After my last touch-ups, she quickly does her own hair. She uses a curling iron to give herself some curls like mine as fast as she can, since we're starting to run a little late for her tastes. When she's done and gets all her stuff back in her bag, we finally start walking over to the hall where all the Sunday school classes are.

She drops me off at the fifth grade classroom, and a lot of kids look at me since I'm someone they've never seen before.

"Hi, Grace," I hear my cousin, Peter, speak. He's sitting at one of the tables, writing on a worksheet. It's nice to see a familiar face. I wish I could sit next to him, but I know I need to go to the girls table, so I take an open seat there. The girls at the table smile at me and introduce themselves. They call me really pretty, which causes my gut to stir uncomfortably. Thankfully, they start talking about today's lesson being about David and Goliath and how we need to trust God, that He's always with us, and His plan will prevail even if it seems impossible. With the conversation changing, the feeling doesn't last a long time.

***

We don't get home from church for a long while because my parents and all the other adults in my family want to talk with everyone. Which leaves me to be very bored because my cousins play with their friends and I have no one. Thankfully, I was allowed to bring *The Merry Adventures of Robin Hood*, so I get to read that.

As I sit in one of the big, comfy chairs in the lobby, I immerse myself in the tales of my hero and how he brings together his band of Merry Men. They all work together and travel all over England, riding horseback and sword fighting and archery. They always have each other's backs, especially Little John, who funnily enough isn't so little.

I can only imagine the green forests of England in the middle ages, riding atop my steed as we gallop through. The wind brushing past as the sunlight breaks through the leaves and the birds chirp in the trees, safe and sound in their nests. At least they're safe, because as Robin Hood would point out, not everyone is.

Out of nowhere, Robin himself, on his own horse, gallops beside me. And on the other side of me comes Little John. They don't say anything, but Robin Hood gives me a knowing smirk. I look behind me to find the rest of the Merry Men behind us, and it excites me to think of going on the adventures with them. Fighting off the Sheriff of Nottingham and his men, helping the poor and needy and giving them the joy they have long needed, and even just sitting around a campfire as Allan a Dale plays music into the night as we all talk and joke and chuckle to ourselves before we drift off to sleep looking at the stars.

Doing all of that sounds like the most amazing thing in the world. Just hanging with a bunch of guys and having such camaraderie and goofing off. They have so much fun in those stories, and I want to have that fun too. I can't wait to have something like that one day.

"Gracie?" Dad's voice breaks through the night's campfire, forcing me to transport back to the lobby of the church. I look up from my book. "Gracie, it's time to head over to Gramma's house. Come on."

Since we're finally leaving, I quickly get up and follow Mom and Dad to the car. Thank God we're going to Gramma's. There, I can finally play with my cousins, and maybe we can play football.

Chapter 3

Dick

"Oh, look at my little granddaughter!" Carol's mother cheers as we walk through the door. The first thing that she does is run up to Gracie and give her the biggest hug. "Oh, you're so much taller than last time, and you're so beautiful."

"Thank you."

"And Carol, you look so lovely yourself."

"Thank you, Mom," my wife says as they share an embrace.

And now it's my turn. My mother-in-law looks at me. "Dick, it's been so long. You look wonderful. How've you been?"

"I've been good."

"Well, why don't you all come inside? Gracie, I know that your cousins are in the family room playing around."

With that, Grace runs inside to go play with them. It makes the three of us chuckle.

"Dick, you and Carol will be in her old room, so you can drop your bags off there."

"Thank you."

I head on upstairs and drop our bags off in Carol's childhood bedroom. Something about coming back to her old room once a year makes me grin. Just seeing her touch all over the room brightens my day. The floral wallpaper and splashes of dark purple just seem to warm my heart. And the posters of hot boy bands from when she was a kid makes me snicker a bit.

As much as I want to dwell around for a little longer, I know better than to keep my wife waiting. Besides, we'll have plenty of time in here later tonight. Maybe we'll even get a little intimate.

I go back down the stairs, but before I can get to Carol, I'm bombarded by her brothers-in-law. "Dick!"

One of them gives me a rough noogie while the other punches me in the shoulder. I make sure to give them a little *what-for* back as we all chuckle.

"How's your year been? Anything exciting?"

"I got a promotion, that's pretty exciting," I joke. Everyone laughs a bit. "Anything exciting for you?"

"Well, the missus is pregnant, so I would say that's a score."

"Really? Congrats to the both of you," I tell him.

"I agree. So should we celebrate with some beers?"

"Only if we can play some football after. Maybe we can let the boys join too," another interjects.

"Long as you don't fall on top of one of them and almost suffocate them."

"I just lost my footing one time, is that really a problem?"

"It was a problem for Robert," I point out.

"It was only for five seconds. Geez."

Doesn't matter what excuse he'll make out of it, we're all going to make fun of him for the one time he landed on top of his nephew.

I feel a tap on my shoulder, and I turn my head to find my sweet, beautiful wife. "Oh, hey."

"Hey. Before you go off with them, mind hanging with me for a while?"

"Not at all."

"Oh, come on, Dick," one of her brothers-in-law jeer. "What about us? You really gonna ditch us for her?"

"Ditch you for my wife? Well, let me think. Yes, yes I would."

Some of them groan.

"You would all do the same. Besides, I'll join you soon enough."

It's enough for them to leave it be. They all go outside and start bringing out the beers. Carol just smiles at me and clings close as she puts her arms around mine. "Thank you."

"Anytime." I give her a small kiss as I quietly hold her hand in mine.

The two of us enter the living room where all of Carol's sisters and her mother are. I assume they're all conversing. Compared to the guys, it's not loud and physical. The ladies are all sitting in their chairs around the room, talking with each other and chortling.

We sit down on the couch, and when we do, all of Carol's sisters compliment how wonderful she looks, and she returns the same sentiments.

"If only you could get Dick to step up his appearance to be like you."

I know they're joshing a bit. "Hey, I do what I can. Not my fault there's so many steps to it."

Some of them giggle. "Yeah, but your hair's a mess."

"I try to make him presentable every day," Carol begins, "but he's often out the door before I can even wake up."

"Well, gotta make sure I'm on time for work. Someone's gotta pick up the garbage," I say.

"Even if he's a little messy, you're lucky to have a man like him, Carol," one of her sisters points out. "I swear, I can barely get David to get to his job on time. And he for sure wouldn't make me breakfast every Sunday."

"It's the least I can do for the love of my life." I beam at Carol. I don't understand how a man wouldn't want to do anything and everything for the prettiest, kindest, smartest, hardest-working woman in the entire world. If anything, I don't do enough for her.

"Speaking of wonderful spouses," another sister speaks up, "Paul and I are going to be having a baby boy!"

Everyone makes their comments of congratulations, including Carol, who quietly clings closer to me.

"Oh my gosh, another boy?"

"Yes, baby number seven's gonna be a boy."

"He's going to be so well loved by you and all his brothers and sisters."

"Have you chosen any names yet?"

"It's not official, but we really like the name Elliot."

"That's such a fun name."

"When's the due date?"

"February twenty-first."

"Aww, he's gonna be a February baby? That's so adorable."

Carol's grip gets a little tighter around my hand.

"Yes, and he might possibly share a birthday with his older sister. Isn't that crazy? If he ends up being a few days early, he might end up being God's birthday present for Hope."

"That would be so sweet."

"Would you all like to see the ultrasound? I'm pretty sure it's in my purse, let me just find it real quick."

"Do you think we can go upstairs?" Carol whispers in my ear. She tries to be discreet about it. Considering how tense and quiet she is, I have an idea of what's going on in her mind.

"Oh, I'm so sorry!" I interrupt the group conversation. "I think I left my phone upstairs. Let me go grab it. Carol, I think I left it in one of your bags, mind helping me?"

My wife nods.

"We'll be back in a few minutes, if that's alright."

"Of course," Carol's mother assures.

The two of us walk upstairs to her old bedroom. Once we're both in that wonderful room, I close the door so that no one can overhear us. My wife helps herself to her own bed.

After making sure that it's as secure as can be, I join Carol and put all my attention on her. "Are you doing okay? Are you gonna be okay?"

I can see the tears welling up in her eyes. "It's... It's just a lot."

"I know." I can see the pain in my wife's heart as she just curls up and cries. It hurts so much to see her like this. Even though I know it's not enough, I hold her in my arms so I can at least give her some comfort. I know what's going through her mind right now and I know what she's feeling. We've talked about it before once, and I know it's even more difficult when it involves a family member.

As she leans on me, I tell her what I tell her every time we go through this. "I love you just the way you are. You're so beautiful and loving to everyone you meet, and I want you to know that I'm happy with having just Gracie. As long as you and her are in my life, I could care less about the number of kids you give me. I just want you, and you're enough." I hope that one of these times it'll finally click in her head that I really don't care. I'm just so happy to have my wife in my life. I don't need anything else. "If anything, you're more than enough. You're so amazing and way out of my league, you might as well be an angel."

It makes her smile a little, and I give her a kiss so I can see that smile grow a bit more. "But are you really sure?"

"Really. You're enough. And Gracie's enough."

"But a son—"

"I don't need a son. I just need what I already have." One of these days, I hope she'll get out of her own head about all of this. She doesn't deserve all the pain she's going through every time she thinks about it. There's gotta be a way to cheer her up. Wait... I got it. "I have something for you."

"Hmm?"

I run to my bag. "Now, I was going to wait to give you this on Christmas, but I think now is a better time." It's her Christmas present, but she needs something to make her joyful and forget everything.

"What is it?" she asks, trying to get a peek from where she sits.

After a moment, I finally find the box and pull it out of my bag. It's so hard to contain my excitement as I go to her and slowly open it, showing the necklace that's inside.

And the second Carol sees it, she forgets everything. "Oh my gosh, it's beautiful! Dick, how did you get this?"

"With my promotion. With all the extra money, it has to go to some place that deserves it."

Carol gently picks it up and runs to the mirror. She puts it on, admiring the metal and gems that shine. What's so rewarding is seeing her smile become as bright as the jewelry she wears.

I sneak up from behind her and whisper, "I love you," into her ear.

"I love you, too." She looks up at me before giving me a loving kiss.

Chapter 4

Robin

racie, aren't you going to help me with the mashed potatoes?" Mom asks. She's getting the potato masher so that we can help make them together. Everyone's in the kitchen helping to make Sunday dinner. Well... all the moms and daughters. The boys get to go outside and play football while the dads all drink beer.

I watch my cousins playing outside, hoping I can go out and play with them. When I was little it was fine, but now I'm "older" so I have to "help make food." Mom says it's so I can learn how to be a grownup and mature, but I don't get why the boys don't have to do it with us. They get to have fun and be like the Merry Men, meanwhile I have to make boring old food.

I try watching my cousins a little longer, seeing them getting ready to hike the ball, but my mom taps my shoulder, so I know I can't get away with it. I just cave in and follow her to the bowl of potatoes and help her mash them up.

After the potatoes are all mashed and we're almost done cleaning up, Gramma comes over. "And how's the food coming over here?" She looks at me when she's asking.

"They're all done."

"Good. Since you guys are all ready and everyone else is finishing up, how about you get the boys to come in for dinner."

"Okay!" Anything to go outside and hang with them.

As fast as I can, I run out the kitchen and out the back door. The porch creaks as I jump down the stairs and go over to my dad and uncles. Since they're a little drunk, I make sure to be mindful of their stumbling. Mom says that men tend to not be aware of their bodies when they're out of it.

"Hey, Dad, dinner's just about ready, and Gramma wants everyone to come in and eat."

"Alrighty, sweetie. We'll be there in a minute."

With that, it's now time to tell my cousins. I walk over to where they're playing, and seeing them just run around with the football tempts me to join. I could just sneak into the line on one of their teams; I doubt they would notice or care. And I doubt any of the dads would care because they're too drunk to pay attention to what's going on.

But Mom might be by the window, and if she sees me go play with them, she'll be pretty mad. I imagine Gramma wouldn't be too happy either, since her and Mom are on the same page.

But playing football would be so much fun! To get muddy and tackle and to throw a ball around. And I bet I can even get a touchdown.

I'm pretty good at sports. I used to play them all the time when I was younger. Back then, I... I just got to play.

I look over at the window. It's a little hard to see with all the kitchen chaos going on inside, but it seems Mom's back is facing me. She's talking to my aunt. And Gramma's nowhere to be seen, so she's probably in a different room.

Which means they wouldn't notice me if I... sneak into the line.

I'm a little nervous, but I'm going for it. As my cousins start lining up for the next play, I run over to Peter, who's in the middle of the field. "What position can I do?"

"You can be the wide receiver if you'd like. The end zone is where the bushes are." He points over to them, and it's a ways away, but I bet I can make it.

I join the line with my other cousins, taking the very end. Like everyone else, I crouch down and get on the balls of my feet, ready to bolt the second I hear Peter call for the ball. One of the boys on the other team starts squaring up on me. I can see the smirk on his face spread, probably because he thinks he's going to tackle me and that it would be easy. I'm going to prove him so wrong.

"Hike!" Peter calls. Immediately, my opponent goes straight for the tackle on me. I knew he was going to do that, so I just hop to the side. He misses me by a mile, and while he lays there eating dirt, I book it for the bushes. All the other boys are focusing on their opponents, so it's the perfect opportunity to score a touchdown.

"Peter! Peter! I'm open!" I make sure to be as loud as I can as I start to approach the end zone. After a moment, we make eye contact, and he throws the ball. I start slowing down a bit—because no way in heck am I gonna not catch it—and follow where it's going, watching it slowly fall and come towards me. As it gets closer and closer, I reach my hands out to grab it.

I feel something wrap around my hips, and before I know it I'm shoved to the ground, someone landing on top of me and making me slide into the dirt. It hurts, but it doesn't suck that much. It's actually kinda fun because it means I really am one of the boys. Getting rough and dirty.

After a minute, my cousin gets up, and then I get up too. That's when I realize I caught the ball and it's still in my hands. "Oh my gosh! I got a touchdown!" I can't believe I actually did that! I actually got to do it and scored!

"Yeah, Gracie!" I hear Peter cheer from the other side of the field, his fists in the air. All the other boys on my team start hooting and hollering as they give me high fives. I join in with them, being as loud and free as I possibly can. We sure are making a ruckus, but it's the best ruckus in the world.

Peter's hand slaps me on the back as he grins. "That was pretty good. You got past Robert!"

"It was pretty easy." And that's the truth.

"Gracie!" I hear Mom's voice, and all of a sudden I can't move. My legs stay right where they are, as if they've been glued to the ground. I can't do anything as my mother comes in a flash. "Oh, Gracie, what happened? Did one of the boys tackle you? Which one of them was it?"

My voice gets caught in my throat. I can't get it out. It's so weird. It's like it has to hop a fence to get out, but can't get high enough to make the jump. I mean, I don't want to tell her that I was playing football; she's not going to be happy if I tell her that, and I just want to make her happy. I don't want to disappoint her.

Mom sees the football in my hands and sighs. Without any words, she gently but firmly grabs my hand and leads me inside to the bathroom. She gets a washcloth and starts dabbing it on my face, washing off the dirt. I want to say something, mostly because it's too quiet for my tastes, but I know she's not happy with me. She saw the football in my hands. I shouldn't talk if she's mad at me, it just escalates.

As she goes down to my dress, she sighs. "Honey, you shouldn't have done that."

"I just wanted to play. What's wrong about—"

"You could've gotten hurt! You were tackled to the ground, your body is not made to go through that. I don't want you to break a bone or worse just because you wanted to play. God didn't make you for that."

"What did God make me for?"

"Well, He made you to be smart, help people, including helping your family with things, and of course He made you to be really beautiful." Mom smiles a bit more when she says that. I hope it grows. Instead, it just disappears. She starts going harder and harder on the dress. "Why is the dirt not coming out?"

I know it's my fault. I shouldn't have played with my cousins. I shouldn't have let the temptation win and sin. "I'm sorry, Mom."

It doesn't help. She just sighs as her hand drops. "Great. Now it's ruined. We're going to have to change you before dinner. Just go and pick something else out from your suitcase, okay? I don't want to deal with this anymore."

I just nod. I'm nervous that anything else I say is just going to make things worse, so I quietly leave and get changed.

After putting on a new dress, it's time for dinner. Thankfully, no one brings up football at the table. Some of my aunts and uncles ask me questions about school and my friends, and I answer them, but other than that I don't really talk. Because of the whole football thing I don't really want to.

Why can the boys play football and I can't? I mean, I know Mom says I just wasn't made that way, but I'm clearly just as good as them and can take a hit. I took it like a champ, and Peter seemed pretty impressed with my touchdown.

Sometimes... sometimes I wish I was born a boy instead of a girl. It's so much more fun to be a boy. You get to have fun and be a little reckless and you get the best band of brothers to bond with and love and do fun stupid things with. It's not fun wearing dresses and having long hair and having to be dainty and having my breasts grow. If anything, all that stuff is... it feels sickening. My head feels like there's a dark cloud surrounding it and like some sort of devil, maybe Satan, is clawing at my skin and trying to painfully peel it off.

I... I don't feel very good.

I must look unwell or something because Dad's getting really concerned. He asks if I can be dismissed from dinner early. Everyone agrees, and Dad picks me up and carries me upstairs to bed. I want to ask him a question, but I can't get it out of my mouth. Something about it feels scandalous to ask. Not even scandalous... sinful and wicked. But I should ask him sometime soon. He would be the only one who would be nice about it and help me.

Dad tells me he loves me and gives me a kiss, like he does every night, and turns the light off as he leaves. As much as I want to sleep, I really can't. There's too much on my mind.

Why did God make me a girl? It honestly feels like some cruel joke.

I don't want to be a girl. I don't want to be some damsel, like Maid Marian. Thankfully, she's not in *The Merry Adventures*, but she's in every other reiteration, always being the one that Robin Hood would wed, and she never does much. She's just some woman who agrees with Robin and someone he loves and that's all she's about. I don't want to be the damsel to be married off; *I* want to be Robin Hood—being the hero and getting the girl.

And it's not like I just want to act like a boy and dress like a boy. I want to *be* a boy. I don't want breasts, I want a flat chest, and to be able to wear my shirt loose or just take it off. I don't want whatever I have down there, I want whatever the boys have. I don't like my body. I don't get why God made me this way.

I wish I could wake up tomorrow and be a boy.

But no, I guess I'm stuck being a girl for eternity.

Chapter 5

Dick

Since it's Christmas Day, we all have to dress nice, as Carol likes to remind me. While she helps Grace get ready, I dress myself up as best I can. I mess with my hair and throw on the dress shirt and blazer my wife got me for this year. The theme is blue and gold for the photo, so she made sure that I am nothing short of it.

"Alright," I hear her voice as she enters the bathroom. "Gracie is all ready for the photo. Now all we need to get ready is you."

"How do I look?" I ask, giving my cocky grin to her. I know what she's going to say.

She giggles a bit. "Let me help you with that."

Carol first starts with my hair, wetting it down and smoothing it out. It takes her a few minutes, but as always, she sure knows how to tame my mess. She turns it from the muddle it is to a sleek and clean hairdo. As a thank you, I give her a kiss. "You're the best wife I could've asked for."

"I know." She looks up at me and smiles. It fills the room and makes my heart swell up, being as beautiful and wonderful as it was the first time I saw it. "Now, come on. We don't want to be the ones they're waiting on."

At her ushering, we go downstairs to the Christmas tree where the rest of the family is gathering. There are still a few people missing, like one of Carol's sisters, but just about everyone else is there. Grace is talking with some of her cousins, looking all beautiful in her new Christmas dress. She's such a wonderful, amazing girl and I'm proud of her. I want to go over to her and ask how her dress fits and how it feels, but Carol's clinging to my arm and not really letting me move too far.

"Alright, everyone, get around the tree for the picture!" Carol's mother comes in with a camera, gently shoving everyone into place. Gramma places us a little further from the tree—since Carol is on the younger end of her siblings—with Grace in front of my wife and I, and my hand on my daughter's shoulder. Now in our perfect positions, Gramma goes to the other families, where she is a lot more specific about what they need to do, going over and physically moving them. The ticking clock in the room slowly creeps its way the next half-hour as Carol's mother keeps moving and changing people's poses. I honestly can't believe it takes us all this long to do one picture.

When the photo's ready, Gramma runs in and joins. A few flashes and camera shutters and it's done. But now it's time for a photo with all the siblings and ones with all of Carol's family and so many other kinds of photos of all the different parents with their kids and families. It's a never-ending photo nightmare. There's not much for us to do until our time, so Gracie and I sit down on the couch as her cousins take turns doing their pictures.

I look over at my daughter, who's just sitting there. I can tell she's just waiting for it all to be over, staring out into the abyss, waiting for her chance to take a photo that I know she doesn't want to do. No kid wants to take these kinds of photos. Hell, I don't like doing these photos. I would like them more if they didn't take so long.

"Hey," I whisper to her. "You having fun?"

"No."

"Neither am I. It's the most boring thing in the whole world." I dramatically flop on the couch a bit, hoping to make Grace laugh and see a smile spread on her face. It works. "Soon enough, we'll be able to eat food and open presents."

"I wonder what presents I got this year. I really hope I got that bow and arrow set I asked for." Just mentioning the bow brings a bigger smile to her face. She's been asking for it for over a year now. Of course, it's because the one and only great Robin Hood is famous for his work with a bow, but considering how long she's wanted it, I think she really wants to learn how to use it. I've even looked at archery lessons for her. Who knows, maybe she could be the best archer in the country. I bet she would put all her focus and energy on it.

I told Carol that we need to finally get her one this year. So knowing that it's probably under the tree waiting for her makes me smile. She's going to be so happy to rip the wrapping off and see it right before her very eyes, just for her. I can't wait to see her learn how to use it and be her own little Robin Hood.

"What do you think you got for Christmas this year?" she asks.

"Probably socks and ties. You know how your grandmother is with clothes."

"I heard that, Richard!" Carol's mother yells from the other side of the room. I won't lie, I sit up a little straighter when she scolds me.

It makes Grace giggle a bit. She makes sure to whisper, "I hope I don't get clothes from Gramma this year. I never really like them, especially the dresses."

"Why don't you like them?"

My little princess starts thinking to herself for a moment. I wait for her to say something, but she never does.

Before I can ask anything about it, or if she would want to talk about it somewhere else, someone interjects. "Dick, is it? I'm Joseph, I don't think we've met before."

I look up to find a man I haven't seen till this morning. Him and one of Carol's sisters drove in earlier today because they were busy up until now. I think he's her new boyfriend. He extends his hand out for a shake, which I take him up on. "Nice to meet you, Joseph."

"Apologies for not being here sooner."

"Oh, that's alright. It's the busiest time of year, after all." I chuckle. It makes him laugh a bit too, thank goodness. I don't like it when people don't smile and laugh. Seeing people not happy always makes me feel terrible because people shouldn't be having to go through that. They should be able to enjoy it all.

"So, how are your folks? Have you seen them yet this Christmas? Or are you guys going to see them after?"

Even though I have said this thousands of times before, I feel uncomfortable about telling an almost pure stranger about my life. Part of it is because I know how it's going to go. It's always the same. "Oh, I don't have any folks."

He's in shock at first and at a loss for words. "Oh... Oh, I'm so sorry. I shouldn't have brought that up."

"No, it's fine."

"How did you lose them? When did it happen?" he asks, now being apologetic and polite, but prodding at the topic as if it's a caged bear in a circus. I'm not surprised by the questions. I often have to answer those kinds of questions.

"A car accident when I was a baby," I lie.

"And you were never adopted?"

"Nope."

"I'm sorry for your loss."

"Eh, it's fine. It happened forever ago. I got other things to focus on, like my sweet wonderful daughter." I give Grace a little bump in the shoulder, which makes her smile. It seems really tight and forced, though. Something's got to be on her mind.

Now that I think about it, I don't think I've seen her have a big smile on her face in a long time. It's always been small and tight for... for quite a long time actually. Why haven't I noticed that before? I really need to sit down and have a talk with her and figure out what's going on.

"Hey, did you guys hear about the new law that's in Congress?" one of Carol's brothers-in-law pipes up as he comes back from his session of photos.

I haven't. I tend to not look at the news because it's too depressing at times.

But Joseph seems very aware. "Yeah. The Families Come First Act?"

"Oh yeah. Good news is that it might actually pass. It's already passed in the House. If it passes in the Senate, then we're all good to go because there's no way the president's gonna veto it."

"What's the Families Come First Act?" I ask. Of course, it sounds important and that it would be very beneficial, but in what way?

"It's a bill that's focused on getting rid of predators and pedophiles. Basically it gives police more access to arresting them."

"Thank God." I've heard about how many of those disgusting devils have been running about free. I'm so glad that something's being done about it. The last thing I want to happen is one of them getting to Grace. I would absolutely lose it if that ever happened. To think that my daughter could be put in that situation...

"I can't believe it took this long for the government to finally wake up and do something about all of it."

"You're telling me." Joseph chuckles. "Seeing all those insane leftists letting criminals run amok was the whole reason why I got into politics in the first place. I mean, imagine having the power to change things, and just making the country—or even the entire world—worse for your own personal gain."

"That's why I can never understand those damn liberals. What's so good about letting terrible people be free all over town? We have laws for a reason! To keep the innocent people safe and the guilty people in prison."

"I mean, why would you abuse and harm children? In any circumstance. It's so vile and revolting, I don't understand how or why any human being can justify doing that," I speak up.

"You and me both."

"Dick! Gracie!" Carol's voice interrupts the conversation. "Come over here, it's time for our photo!" My wife waves us over to the tree, so my daughter and I walk over and get ready to take a photo for five seconds and be done. Five seconds, unfortunately, turns into ten minutes of Gramma yelling at us to move an inch to the left, then an inch to the right, complaining about how I somehow wrinkled my blazer, and Grace not standing straight enough.

"Come on, Grace. Just stand tall and roll your shoulders back," Gramma instructs.

Grace tries to, but her shoulders always seem to somehow fall forward. The way her back curves honestly looks uncomfortable.

"Alright. Grace, loosen up a bit. And then just throw your shoulders back."

She tries again, but her shoulders end up going even further in front of her. It's so weird. It's not that hard to stand up straight.

"Carol, get your daughter to fix her posture."

"Gracie, come on. It's one photo. All you have to do is stand tall."

"But I am," my daughter whines. It's a lie, and even she knows it, but why would she lie about it? What's stopping her from having proper posture? She's acting like it would kill her.

Carol gently grabs Grace's shoulders and brings them all the way back, to the point where her shoulders are touching her mother. It looks uncomfortable, but what looks the most painful about it is Grace's face. She looks like she's about to burst into tears.

"Perfect! Alright, everyone, smile!" We all do, including my daughter who's fighting the urge to cry. There's a few flashes of light blinding us, and finally all our photos are done. Praise the Lord that we, eventually, got that over with.

Shortly after, the whole family eats the dinner the girls made, and then it's time for presents. As I expect, all I get is socks and ties. Grace, on the other hand, is a lot more excited. She gets new dresses and her very own straightening iron. But what she seems the most thrilled about is the bow-and-arrow-shaped present under the tree that has her name on it. I can barely wait myself because I know how joyful she's going to be when she unwraps it and sees that glorious thing before her.

It takes a while for it to finally get in her hands, and when it does, I can tell that she just wants to rip it open. She's bouncing up and down where she sits as she asks, "can I open it now?"

"Wait for your cousin to open his, then it's your turn," Gramma chides in.

Grace sits there and intently watches her cousin open the new pocket knife he got. He receives lots of wows and love for the present and thanks his parents for it, and then it's Grace's turn. She tears the wrapping paper like she's a wild animal about to eat her prey. It makes me laugh to see a bit of the sweet, wonderful Gracie I know. And any moment, she's going to be losing it over the fact that she finally got the bow she's been asking for. "What'd you get, kiddo?"

Her face falls. "A set of bows." She raises up a shiny brand new hair bow in defeat.

Wait... "What?"

"What kind of bows did you get? Did you get some sparkly ones?" Gramma asks with a grin.

"I don't know."

"Oh, you know what they are. There's a red one, a sparkly purple one, and look at this one! It has your name embroidered on it and everything!" Gramma shows off a bow, which is very pink and has "Gra-cie" written in a pretty cursive. "Now, what do you say?"

"Thank you," Grace says to Carol and I, though the frown on her face says otherwise.

"You're welcome, sweetie." Carol speaks as if our daughter's sentiment was sweet.

"Honey," I begin. "I thought we were getting her a bow set."

"Yes, and that's what I got her."

I thought I was specific about it being a bow and some arrows, but now I'm starting to wonder if I had made it up. But that wasn't the case—we had talked about this before. "I meant like a bow set for archery. She's been wanting one for forever."

"I could've sworn you meant a set of new bows. Besides, that's dangerous. She could poke her eye out with that. I don't want her to get hurt."

"I mean, yeah, it can be dangerous, but that's why we would take her to lessons. She would learn how to use it properly so she doesn't get hurt."

"We'll talk about this later. Right now, let's just enjoy Christmas, alright?"

I'm not happy about it, but at the same time, I know we probably shouldn't argue in front of everyone, especially in front of Grace. "Okay," is what I utter, but looking at Grace and how sad she is, I don't feel okay. I feel like I'm not being a good father, and I know a bit about what it's like to feel disappointed in your father.

Chapter 6

Dick

 tuck Gracie in, which I'm glad I can do. Carol wants to hang out with her sisters and parents more, so it gives me an excuse to have a private conversation with my daughter.

I try to make it like usual because I don't want to stress out my daughter or freak her out more. So I crack the same jokes and tuck her in tight. "So that none of the monsters can rip you out of bed," I tell her.

Grace sighs. "Dad, I'm eleven, not five."

"Oh, but those monsters are still very real at eleven."

"They're not. I'm almost a teenager, Dad."

I guess she's right about that. She's growing up so fast, and she's going to be so independent soon. I'm not ready for it.

"Goodnight, Dad."

"Goodnight, Gracie," I say, somewhat not wanting to talk about what's making her off. Just telling her goodnight, I can see her shrink further into the covers, as if she's trying to hide herself, or trying to not look.

Inside me, I feel the dread sneak up into my gut. The idea of sitting down and having a serious conversation with my child makes me uneasy. I don't know what we're going to talk about, and I don't know what's been eating at her. Has someone been trying to pressure her into doing drugs? Did I say something wrong? Did someone sexually assault her? Is she having intrusive thoughts? Is she hurting herself? Does... Does she want to end her life?

As much as I'm scared about the conversation, I know that it needs to happen. For her, I need to get over my fear of the talk and just have it. I need to have it for her. "Hey, Gracie?"

"Yeah?"

I start feeling a little light-headed. "Can... can we talk for a second?"

She's quiet. I fear that she's going to shoo me off without me being able to figure out what's wrong. Thankfully, she asks, "what is it?"

My heart starts going a hundred miles a minute. "I can tell that something's bothering you. You've been a little off today."

"Is this about the photos?"

"No! No, it's not about the photos, I promise. I couldn't care less about those." It's partially the truth. I truly couldn't care less about the photos. The situation is about that moment, though. "I know you've been off a little more recently, and *I know that Mom always chocks it up to hormones*, but I just want to ask how you're feeling, and a bit why you're feeling that way."

Grace looks at me, but she doesn't say anything. How do I get her to tell me? I just want to make sure that she's fine; how do I make sure of that?

"I love you very much, and I just don't want anything bad to happen to you. That's all. And if you want to talk, what happens in this room stays between us, alright?"

Grace nods.

"Would you like to tell me, or do you not want to talk about it right now?"

Her gaze falls to the floor, and I expect her to whisper that she wants to be left alone. It's a surprise when she asks, "why was I born a girl?"

I don't know how to answer. "What do you mean?"

"Why was I born a girl and not a boy?"

Oh... how do I answer this? "I... I don't know. I guess God just decided that you were going to be a girl."

"How do we know that God decided? What if Satan switched it at the last minute?"

"I don't think Satan does that. Besides, everything that happens is God's plan. Right down to a tee."

"Like all the wars that are happening? And innocent people that get killed in terrorist attacks? And all the kids that die when a gunman comes to school?"

Even though my instinct is to say that all of those things are part of God's plan, it... it never really hit me that if everything is God's plan, that it must also be His plan and will that all those people die. Especially those kids that were just going to school and trying to learn. They had done nothing wrong, in fact, their sins were incomparable to probably a lot of adults that were in their lives.

"But God would never have that in His plan," my daughter points out. She knows what I'm thinking. "Because He's supposed to be all good and wonderful and wants all of us to live in harmony, right?"

That part seems a little easier to get behind, but I'm still a little in shock about the first part. "You're right."

"I... I just think that God made a mistake."

"What kind of mistake?"

Grace becomes quiet, and I can tell she's struggling to get the words out her mouth. "I think..." She starts getting really quiet. "I think God meant to make me a boy."

"What makes you think that? Is it because you like to do more boyish things? If so, there are a lot of girls that like to do boyish things."

"No, it's not that. It's... like it didn't matter as much when I was younger, but now that I'm growing and my body's changing, I hate it. My chest is growing and every time I look in the mirror and see it, I start feeling sick and I feel like something's crawling all over my skin in a disgusting and creepy way, like if a bunch of spiders started skittering all over me. And when I wear a dress, it feels even worse. I want to claw at my skin to get rid of it, but then it never goes away and I'm just itching myself. My whole body just feels terrible and I hate it! If I was a boy, it would be so much better because I wouldn't have these things on my chest and I wouldn't have to wear dresses. And I could play in the mud and not get yelled at and I wouldn't have to spend all day cooking and having to be polite and sociable and pretty and dainty and all that other dumb stuff Gramma and Mom keep harping about!"

I don't know what to say. I don't know how to react, or even how to digest this information. Can that one thing be what's making all this fuss? How do I help her with this? It's not what I was expecting. "Is that why you've been off recently?"

Grace nods.

"That and only that?"

"Dad, I'm being honest. Take it seriously!"

"I am, kiddo. I just want to make sure," I calmly tell her, doing my best to make my voice sound soft but firm. "Is it really that bad? That being a girl makes you feel like that?"

She nods. "And sometimes it makes me feel super sick. Like... like yesterday when I had to leave dinner early. It was because of that."

"Really? It made you sick?"

"Yeah..." She hides under her covers a bit more after saying that, her eyes and above being all I can see.

"What kind of sick? Like the feeling was so much that it made you sick?"

"Yeah."

"I see." I'm still trying to wrap my head around it all. I think I'm getting a bit of a start. It's not perfect, but it's... it's something to start with.

"You believe me, right, Dad?" My kid looks at me with such innocence, and I know just by looking into my child's eyes that my little baby needs me in this moment, and that I need to be the person who's there for them and supports them. Even if I don't understand what exactly my kid is going through, the least I can do is trust them and do my best. They wouldn't lie to me, and it's for my child's health. I want my kid to be the best person they can be, and that starts with me.

"I do. And I'm going to help you so you get all better. Is there anything I can do to help you feel better?"

For the first time, Grace's mind goes blank. She hasn't thought this far. "I don't know."

"Well, if you think of things, can you tell me so I can do that?"

"Yeah." She smiles a bit at the idea. It looks different than it usually does though. In a good way.

"Alright then. Goodnight, kiddo. Love you." I give her a kiss on the forehead, this time hoping she knows that I am always here for her and that I mean it when I say I love her. Slowly, with the weight of her emotions on my shoulders, I get up and start walking out.

"Wait, Dad."

"Yes?"

"Can... can you not tell Mom?"

"Why's that?"

"I'm scared of how she's gonna react. I don't know how she's going to feel about it, or what she's going to do, or—"

"Grace, it's okay! It's okay." I try to calm her down. I don't want to put any more stress on my kid.

"I'm just not ready for her to know yet. Can you please not tell her?"

That makes me a little sad to hear. I don't really like the idea of not telling my wife something, especially something involving our child. It feels like I would be keeping a terrible secret from the love of my life. But... if it's for my kid, it's probably okay. And it's not like I would be keeping the secret for long. Once Grace is comfortable with it, then we can all talk about it and figure out what's best for our kid. "Sure."

"Thank you."

"You're welcome." I try to give her my best grin. It makes her a little less tense, thank goodness. "Love you."

"Love you, too. Goodnight."

I make sure she's all comfortable and asleep before leaving her room, and even though she seems at ease, I start to feel a little unsettled about everything.

I do my best to act like everything's normal and fine and just get ready for the night. My wife doesn't really catch on, thankfully. I must look pretty normal if she doesn't say anything. She puts on her nightgown and kisses me goodnight, only smiling and being blissfully unaware of my guilt or how our child's feeling ill from her own emotions.

As she's falling asleep, I realize I probably won't be getting any sleep tonight. My poor kid plagues my mind, and the idea of harboring things from my spouse makes an anxious ball in my stomach form. It's very clear that it's going to be a long night.

I pull out my phone and just look for something to do. I start scrolling through some random posts about everyone's Christmases with their families, but I keep thinking back to Gracie. There's got to be a way I can help her figure out what she's going through. Maybe I can search up her symptoms and find something to go off of. Anything that can help me be there for her.

How would I even search this? Why does my skin feel itchy? Why does it feel like something's crawling up my skin? Why do I want to be a boy? Why does my daughter say she's a boy? Yeah, we can start with that.

I type it into the search bar and hold my breath a bit, a little afraid of the answer that I'm seeking out. I'm a little surprised to see the red banner right below the bar saying that I'm looking at explicit content. All of a sudden, I grow confused and worried about what my kid is going through.

My screen bombards me with different websites, each claiming how their daughter said the same things. They seem rather old, dating about four years or so back. I want to click on one and learn some more, but I'm a little hesitant. What would the answers be?

One of the suggested "asked questions" pops out to me. It says something that feels a little more medical, so it feels less biased than all the other ones that have parents sounding concerned or like their children had enrolled in Satan's army. It says, "what is it called when a girl thinks she's a boy?"

I click on it, and it brings up something by the name of "gender dysphoria". The website itself isn't an American one, but at the same time, it seems the only one that approaches the topic from an actual health standpoint. So I fall deeper and deeper into the hole that is "gender dysphoria."

Gender dysphoria is a terrible feeling that someone gets when they feel that their body and appearance doesn't correlate with their gender identity.

Why does that word sound familiar? Gender identity...

Symptoms of gender dysphoria include discomfort, withdrawing themselves from social events, anxiety, depression, and thoughts of self-harm or suicide.

Oh gosh... is that what my little baby is going through? Is it so bad that my kid is depressed or might kill themself?

I need to find out more. How can I help my kid? How can I make sure that it doesn't get to a point where they don't want to live?

I spend the whole night scrolling on my phone, learning all that I can about the topic of "gender identity."

Chapter 7

We drive home the next morning, and a few weeks pass after that sleepless night. I've only been able to sleep once every few days, which my wife's been concerned about. I feel bad that she's worrying over me. The last thing I want to do is cause my wife distress, but I also don't want to put my child in an uncomfortable situation that they don't want.

The nice thing is that Grace has been getting more and more comfortable with me. She confided in me when we got home that she wants to wear pants and shirts more, and asked if I can talk to Mom about it. I promised her I would, but I haven't really gotten around to it with work and Carol being busy with chores around the house. Before I know it, my spouse is asleep in our bed and I feel more and more awful about not being able to have the conversation for my child and be more open about things with my wife.

What makes things worse is that Grace has gotten a little sicker recently. She threw up and had to miss school today because of it.

"Hey, Dad," my daughter asks me as I'm tucking her into bed that evening. "I have another thing I want to try."

"What is it?"

"Do you think that maybe I can go by a different name?"

"Why's that?"

"Grace is a very girly name. I don't like it when you guys call me that. It's kinda the same feeling I get when I have to wear dresses."

"I see." I can't believe she's felt like this so much and so often. Honestly, it just shows how strong and brave she is. I can't believe she's had to deal with it this long. Eleven years is a long time to deal with that level of pain, especially when your name is used so often every single day. "Is there anything you have in mind that you want us to call you?"

"No. I was hoping that maybe you can choose something."

"Me? Why me? This is about you."

"But I want you to choose my name. My only ask is that it's a guy name, of course."

"Oh, yes, of course." I have to think for a minute. I could've waited till tomorrow, but I know this is too important to put off. Especially with how my child looks at me so eagerly. I have never seen her with such excitement. She's practically bouncing in her bed.

What kind of name would suit my kid? Well, rather, if I had a son, what would I have named him? We knew Gracie's gender—no, sex —before we started coming up with names, so it's not like I can try and pull one from there. I don't know if Grace would've been a fan of that anyway.

I can look up the meanings of names and find ones that I feel would describe my kid so well. Something about being brave or a hero. Or maybe I can name my kid after someone I admire. It's dumb, but it's something I can get away with, and my kid clearly wants me to name them.

Out of the blue, the perfect name dawns on me. "What about Robin?"

My child's eyes light up. "Like after Robin Hood?"

"No, after Robin Williams."

"Robin Williams? Who's that?"

"Robin Williams was one of the best comedians to ever live! I've shown you stuff he's in."

"Like what?"

"Like... oh which ones have I shown you? *Jumanji*? That one movie about the board game?"

"I don't remember that one."

"But I've shown you *Hook*, right? It's the one where Peter Pan grew up."

"I definitely would've remembered it if I had seen it."

Wow. Have I really not shown her anything that my favorite comedian has done? I could've sworn there was something.

"Dad, he sounds like a cool guy and all, but can I be named after Robin Hood, please?"

I make sure to be very dramatic in my sigh, which makes my kid giggle a bit. "Fine, you're named after Robin Hood."

"Yes!"

"But your middle name is going to be William, right?"

"No, Dad. I want it to be Perseus."

"Alright, alright, fine. It'll be Perseus."

That makes my kid smile.

"Well then, goodnight. Robin."

I look at my little Robin, and they have the biggest smile on their face.

"And can you call me a boy?"

"Like what exactly?"

"Like *boy, he, sir, him, his, son.* Those kinds of things."

"Yeah, of course, kiddo."

"Thanks. But also don't do it in front of Mom quite yet."

"I won't." It hurts, but it's also for my dau—no, my son. It's for my son and I want him to be happy and healthy. I give him a kiss on the forehead, and he has a smile on his face. It's that smile that's a little bit different. It's getting bigger and bigger.

My son turns on his side and goes to sleep. I watch him a little bit longer before I leave his room.

Walking into the kitchen, I find my wife in there and cooking up some soup for herself. I don't think she's noticed me, which means I can surprise her. As quiet as I can possibly be, I slowly start sneaking up to her, making sure her back is always faced towards me. I get closer and closer, her focus still on the soup. It doesn't take long to be behind her. I wait a second, then wrap her up in a hug. "Boo!"

It makes Carol laugh. "Nice try, Dick, but I knew you were there."

"How?"

"I could see you in the window." She giggles. Looking at the glass in front of us, I can see our reflection. I guess she did have that for her.

"Fine. You win."

"I know." A little smug smirk spreads on her face. "Do you want any soup? I think I made a little too much."

"Yeah, sure." Even though the soup smells good, it's not really on my mind. It may fill the room, but Robin is what fills my mind. I still haven't asked Carol if our kid could wear pants. Now can be a good time—Carol and I are both very awake, and I know my wife is in a happy mood. It's the best time to have a rational conversation about it.

All of a sudden, I start feeling very hot, and I feel like my stomach is knotting itself together as if it's the yarn on Gramma's knitting needles. Why am I so nervous? It's not like Carol would freak out. She's very smart and level headed, and I'm sure with some of the research I've done, she'll understand.

"Uh... Carol?"

"Yes?"

"I... I was talking with..." Oh, I've got to remember to use the right—well, wrong—name! "With Gracie." I feel so terrible for calling him that, even if it's what he wants right now. "And... and she was telling me that he—she wants to start wearing pants."

Carol becomes oddly stiff at the mention of pants. The knots start getting tighter. "What?"

"I mean, she used to wear them a lot, and you let her, she just wants to go back to them."

"I let her wear some overalls, but other than that, she has worn dresses and only dresses since she was four."

"Well, why can't she wear pants like she did when she was a baby?"

"Because it's not lady-like. And back then, things were a lot different. For the worst, I might add. What we have now is perfect. We live in the most wonderful place, we are well off and have a roof over our heads, and the country's finally getting laws passed to make things better. It's not like when you were a kid, everything's finally getting better."

"Our kid told me that they don't like wearing dresses. It's making them sick. They need to wear pants."

"What kind of sickness is caused by not wearing pants? That's absolutely absurd. Do you hear yourself?"

"I just think that we should let her wear pants. What's the worst that comes out of it? That she gets better? You can't deny that she's getting sick and that it's getting worse. She's missed school because of it, Carol."

"It's because it's her time of the month, that happens. You just don't understand because you're a man, and pants are definitely not going to fix it."

"Can we at least just try it? We're not in their body, we don't know what's going on, only Grace does, and she probably knows what she needs."

"She's eleven, she doesn't understand what she needs and doesn't need yet. She still has some growing up to do. It's not like one day she's your little baby and the next she's a grown adult—there's an in-between."

"Why can't you just give her one? Just let her do what she needs to do! One pair of pants isn't going to do anything!"

"It's the first step to the road to Hell, and I am not putting my daughter on that path. It starts with pants, then it goes to mutilating her own body and becoming a prostitute and one of those transsexuals. Do you want your sweet little girl to become that? Because I don't! I want her to be safe and healthy!"

But denying him that simple thing is what makes him go farther and farther away from being safe and healthy! I can't understand what's going on. It's just one lousy pair of pants. Why can't we give that to him? He just wants to be comfortable and himself. As his father, I want to—I *need* to—supply that for him. I... I just don't understand why Carol won't let him. Carol, of all people, who loves everyone and is so kind and sweet and just wishes that everyone be safe and healthy and have a roof over their head and food on the table. Why won't my wife, why won't the one person I love and know so much, do the thing that made me first fall in love with her?

When I was struggling in college because I had no family and poor grades and a job that couldn't even feed me, and she saw me and gave me some of her lunch because I looked so frail. The Carol that invited me to her family's Sunday dinner because she wanted to make sure I had a real meal at least once a week. The Carol that bought me new shoes when she saw that the sole was almost completely off my old ones. The Carol who loved me and made her family take me in because I was just tossed around between foster homes all my life and never had a proper family.

Why... Why is she acting like this? Where's the Carol I know? Where's the Carol I love and married?

Carol is still the same person, though. It's not like people change in a snap. Maybe she's just misunderstanding; maybe I need to explain myself better.

"How about we take her to the doctor? To just make sure that Gracie isn't... isn't coming down with something bad," I speak up.

"I told you, it's probably just cramps."

"Just... I want to make sure she's safe and healthy too, and I just think she's coming down with something. Let's just take her to the doctor to make sure, okay?"

Carol is quiet for a moment, but she can understand where I'm coming from. "Okay. I'll call the office tomorrow morning, and we'll see when they can take her in."

Praise the Lord that Carol listens to that. Hopefully when we take him to the doctor, they can diagnose Robin with gender dysphoria, and then hopefully we can get him some help from there. "Thank you," I tell my wife, but she seems a little annoyed with me. She doesn't say anything back.

Chapter 8

Robin

A few days after Mom and Dad's fight, I wake up and Mom tells me we're going to the doctor. I've been feeling a lot sicker and have thrown up every day. And when it came to the pants, she reacted like I thought she would. That's just about pants. I can't imagine how she would react about me wanting to cut my hair, or just calling me Robin.

Mom did start getting a little more concerned about me since I started throwing up. I can see the worry in her eyes and the way her brows knit together. I feel a little bad making her worry, but at the same time, it's kind of her fault. She's causing it, whether or not she knows it. I'm not angry at her for it, though. I'm... I'm not exactly sure how I'm feeling.

I mostly feel sick right now, but I also feel really sad. The sadness and the sickness kind of intertwine together, like a braid. There's also another emotion somewhere in there. Like anger... but I could never be angry at my mother. I know she loves me, even if she's not doing the right things for me. I would say... I would say I'm frustrated. Dad understands, or is doing his best to understand what I'm going through. Why can't Mom do the same? They both love me very much, and even though I knew that these were going to be their reactions to it all, they went two different ways with it.

"Alright, Gracie, we're here. Do you think you can walk?"

"Yeah," I lie. The reality is that I feel like if I move, I'm going to throw up, but considering that I haven't really eaten this morning, there's nothing to throw up.

"Alright, come on, then."

I get out of the car and we both walk into the hospital. While Mom checks in with the nurse, I sit down and do my best to be present. Closing my eyes helps a bit, since I can rest but be aware of everything going on. Even though all I can see is darkness, it helps to focus more on Mom's voice so I know when the doctor's here.

It takes a while, but a nurse calls my name, and Mom and I go to a room where they do all the check-up stuff. She weighs me, notes my height, checks my heartbeat, and a few other things. She also asks Mom some questions, such as if I've had my first period yet. Mom says yes, which is a lie. It's not like she knows it's a lie, she just really thinks that the reason I'm sick is because I must've had my first period. Thankfully, I haven't yet, but I don't understand why she doesn't ask me. She just assumes that must've been the reason.

The nurse leaves, and Mom stands next to the bed and rubs my shoulder. Because I'm feeling so out of it, I lean on her. "Don't worry, Gracie," she tells me. "The doctor will be here soon, and then hopefully we'll know what you have and can get some medicine for you."

Whatever the doctor's going to give me, I doubt it's going to work. Dad told Mom what I need, and she denies it. She doesn't understand how simple the solution is. Unlike Dad, though, I knew she was probably going to say that and why she said that. Dad must've paid more attention to his research for me than church every Sunday. He told me I probably had gender dysphoria, which is commonly found in people whose gender differs from their sex. I may not be exactly sure what it is or what it's going to lead to, but I have a feeling that it's something a lot of Christians, including Mom, don't like.

"Hello, Grace," the doctor says as he comes in. "How are you feeling today?"

"Not well."

"So I've heard. Do you feel well enough to listen?"

I shake my head. I can probably listen, but I don't want to be expected to pay attention. I'd rather act like I'm out of it and secretly hear what he has to say.

"Alright then. Mrs. Wright, there is definitely something that Grace has come down with. We're not entirely sure what it is, but it doesn't seem like it's cancer or anything extremely serious. I'm assuming it's just the flu."

"She's never had the flu this bad."

"My guess is there's some other factor in play, like maybe an infection of some sort. Either way, I would suggest getting her to eat some food. She's lost a lot of weight from throwing up and is behind for her age. As for the flu, just pick up some flu medicine from the drug store and it should go away in a few days with some proper rest."

But it won't. Because that's not what I have. I don't know what exactly it is, but I expected the doctor to say something other than the flu. A doctor's supposed to know what's wrong with me and tell me how to fix it. How can he overlook my throwing up out of nowhere and my loss of weight to a cold? I don't even have a fever or a runny nose!

"Well, alright, then," Mom sighs. I can tell she's not happy with the answer. She thought there was going to be one, but there wasn't. "Can you write the prescription so I can pick it up on the way home?"

"Yes, Mrs. Wright. I'll get that for you right now."

With that, he leaves to get one, and Mom tries to be comforting. "Don't worry, Gracie, we're going to get some medicine for you and you'll be all better."

As her hand rubs my shoulder, I get an odd sensation. It feels like her hand's leaving a stinging goo on me. I want to tell her to stop touching me because I don't like the feeling and it kinda hurts, but I'm not really strong enough to say much. And I don't want to hurt her feelings.

***

"What?"

"The doctor said it's probably just the flu. I mean, it seems like more than the flu to me, Dick, but we should trust the doctor and give her the medicine."

"She doesn't have the flu! What did the doctor say?"

Dad and Mom are arguing again. I hate hearing them yell. Even though I know nothing comes from it, hearing Mom raise her voice always makes me nervous. I'm not even in the room and I'm afraid. The blankets on my bed are my only comfort from her anger as I curl up under them.

"He said that it's for sure not cancer, but she has a lot of symptoms that follow the common cold."

"This is not a cold."

"He said it might be a little more inflated due to an infection of some sort. That's all that I know, Dick, so let's just follow his orders and give her the medicine. If she doesn't get better in a couple days, then we'll take her back and get her checked again."

"It is not the flu, it's not anything like that."

"Oh really? How would you know? You're not a doctor. You're a garbage man."

"I used my brain and the internet. She does not have a cold, she does not have the flu, and medicine isn't going to help her!"

"Well, if you're so smart, then what is it, Dick? What's going to get her better?"

"I told you: pants."

Mom moans.

"Pants are going to get her better. I know it sounds dumb but you have to at least try it. It can't hurt anyone, it's just clothes, and when she gets better, you're going to see it and it's going to help all of us."

"Shut up about your stupid pants!"

"This is about our child, Carol. We need to do what's best for them! And if not pants, let her cut her hair short, let her change her name, let her just do something so that she can feel like herself!"

"No! She is not doing any of those things! That's how you go down the devil's path, and I am not letting my daughter do that. I am not going to watch her destroy herself. What kind of mother would I be to let her do that?! What kind of mother would I be to not teach her right from wrong or to push her in the wrong direction?! I need to be there for her and help her!"

"You're already destroying Robin—you're hurting our son!"

"I am..." It all of a sudden gets very quiet.

I can't breathe.

Dad... Oh, Dad, what have you done?

"What did you say?" Mom's tone darkens, and I can't hold back my tears.

Dad can't figure out a way to twist it.

I know he didn't mean to, I know it slipped.

But now I'm so scared. What's going to happen? What's she going to do to me?

"You bastard! You terrible no-good bastard! You're the reason Gracie has been like this." When she says that horrid name, I feel like she's stabbing me in the heart. "You filled her head with fantasies of Robin Hood and all these adventures! I should've never let you get that book for her. You've made her think she can be like Robin Hood: that she can be some boy that travels around the world and 'saves people'. Gracie doesn't need to be Robin Hood, she needs to be Gracie! She needs to understand that there's no evil government to fight and most of all that she is not a boy or a man. I'm sorry I couldn't give you a son, Dick, alright? But that doesn't mean that you should go and force her to be one!"

"Carol, I didn't care if he's a boy or a girl when they were born, and I don't care now, you—"

"I don't want to hear another word out of you! You screwed our daughter up so bad that she's sick and frail! She looks up to you and you used that to turn her into the child you wanted! You're sick in the head for doing that! You confused her! I should've known all those years ago when you were the same. For forcing our little Gracie to be something she's not, for forcing our little Gracie to sin! You're a pathetic excuse of a man, let alone a father! I should've known when you told me about your parents! I should've known when you were confused so long ago! You're just like them—you're not any better! I should've listened to my mother—the apple doesn't fall far from the tree! People don't change. You ruined your child's life, and she might never recover from this!"

"Carol—"

"No, don't you dare! I don't care how much you love me or how much you care about our daughter! After what you've done to her, you can't fool me! I don't want you anywhere near her, all you'll do is make things worse! You'll make her sicker and sicker and make her drown in sin with it! How far has this gone? Have you mutilated her? Have you injected her with drugs?"

"Carol, that's not how—"

"Tell me what you've done to her!"

"I've only called him by a different name and a boy!"

"Oh, you're such a disgusting excuse of a father, confusing your own child for your personal gain! She's only eleven—think of how much corruption you've caused by making her believe those things at a young vulnerable age!"

"Carol, where are you—Carol!"

The footsteps start getting louder and louder. I wish that it's only because she's getting angrier, but I know that they're just coming closer and closer.

The door slams against the wall of my room as her feet make the whole ground shake. Mom grabs my shoulder and turns me over so I have to face her. Her nails dig through my clothes and into my skin as she sees me curl up with tears in my eyes. A teardrop falls down my cheek in its already paved path.

Even though there's so much anger and tension in her body, there are tears in her own eyes. I don't like that she's sad because of how she's treating Dad. I know those tears are for me and only me, and the fact that she holds so much sadness in one hand and so much anger in the other makes me so afraid that I feel like I'm in paralysis.

"Gracie, did you hear what I said?"

I didn't even catch that she spoke to me.

"Did *he* do anything to you?"

I have to speak, I need to speak for Dad. I need to stand up for him! Mom would trust me, she believes me. I need to defend him! "He's been calling me Robin and a boy, but I asked him to do that! It's not his fault. I asked him."

"Robin," I hear Dad from the door, but I can't see him. "I'm so sorry."

"Shut up!" Mom turns around to scream at him. "She's going to turn into one of those transsexuals because of you!"

"Transsexuals?"

"Get out! Get out of my house! You and your disgusting ideologies!"

"Carol—" Before Dad can say anything more, Mom pushes him out of my door frame.

"You just want to torture your own child and experiment on her! You're a disgusting perverted freak of nature, you bastard! You're a no-good son of a whore who can't think beyond what he wants and how it's ruining everything else around you! I hope you're happy with what you did because you're never going to see Gracie again! I'm going to call the police and tell them about all of this and have you rot in jail for what you did to my daughter! I'm going to fix her and make sure she gets the proper help and doesn't go down that wretched hole that everyone in your family has gone down. She's not going to end up like you, or your parents, or your grandparents because she is *my* daughter!"

I hear the front door crash into something and a thud. What scares me more is hearing Dad moan in pain.

I want to run to the front door, but I don't have the energy or strength to get out of bed, let alone move.

"Carol, can we please just have a calm conversation, all three of us?"

"Leave this house right now, or I'm calling the police! Get in your dinky little truck and never come into my life again!"

"Carol—"

Something shatters into thousands of pieces as I lay helpless and in pure terror. I'm scared that Mom's gonna get the gun.

I think Dad is too because I hear the engine of the old truck, and it slowly gets quieter and quieter and quieter...

Chapter 9

Robin

s Dad had said, the medicine doesn't make me any better.

I miss Dad.

I haven't seen him in a week.

After Mom says goodnight, I cry because I just wish Dad was here. I wish I could still hear his voice say "goodnight, Robin." I miss his jokes, and looking at the stars with him, and talking about Robin Hood. Even our arguments I wish were still around. They were never big arguments, but they did annoy me... at the time.

I wish I could hear *my* name.

As if that wasn't bad enough, the kids at school heard what happened with Dad, and even though I've only felt good enough to go for two separate days, the first day being back was hard. They called him a bastard and a pervert. I don't know what those words mean, but I doubt it's good things. My classmates definitely don't know the extent of it all, but they'll blurt out what their parents say. One of them asked if my Dad had groomed and molested me. A kid spoke for me and said that was what happened.

I asked the teacher if I could sit in the corner the second day.

The third day I'm feeling kinda well. After Mom makes sure that I'm healthy enough to walk around, she serves up some eggs and bacon for me. "Please help yourself. You need to eat all you can."

She's been saying that for the past few days. It scares me a bit when she says that.

I slowly take my fork and begin eating my breakfast. I only get a few bites of egg and half a strip of bacon down before I start feeling nauseous. There's no way I can eat any more without vomiting everywhere.

A part of me hopes Mom won't notice or say anything, but I see her eyes glued to my plate in passing, and I know that I have to speak up because of it. "I can't eat anymore. I don't feel very good."

"Gracie, you need to gain some weight. You are so frail right now, you're practically bone, and let me tell you that is very unhealthy."

I didn't choose to be like this. I don't want to be like this! "If I eat, I'm gonna throw up."

"Listen, Gracie." Mom grabs my hands and looks into my eyes so closely that I can't look anywhere else. I feel trapped in her gaze. Nothing I can do will get me away from her trance. "What's going on right now is not healthy. You shouldn't starve yourself to be skinny. Those princesses you see in the movies are not realistic. And you should never try to be that size."

What? I don't want to be a princess! I never wanted to be a princess and I never will want to be a princess! I don't like what's going on right now! I want to be a prince! Or Robin Hood! And I just want to be able to eat and not throw it up almost immediately!

"Now, open your mouth. You're going to eat this."

"Mom, I can't—" Before I can finish what I'm saying, she stabs some food with the fork and shoves it into my mouth. As the runny egg goes down my throat, I get so scared that it's going to come right back up. Mom's gonna be so mad at me if I do.

She tries to put more food down my mouth, but I close it before she can get there. "Grace, open your mouth."

I shake my head.

I expect her to order me to open my mouth again, but instead she grabs my face and forces my mouth open just so she can put food in it. I think about spitting it out or not swallowing, but the fact that she's right in front of me and has my face in her hands makes me feel like there's no choice but to have it go down the hatch.

Despite my silent cries the next few minutes, she does it again and again until all the food on the plate's gone. At this point, I'm expecting the barf to slowly drip out like a bucket that's filled with too much water. There's no way I'm going to be able to keep it together.

"Now that you've eaten, it's time to get dressed. We're going somewhere today."

The way she says it confuses me. Even though it feels impossible to speak without barf about to spew out, I'm able to muster some words. "Are we not going to school today?"

"I'm going to take you to a different kind of school."

I start feeling even more woozy. What kind of different school are we going to? Am I going to have to go there now instead of regular school? If I'm really going to a new school, I need to be at my best. I'm nervous to ask Mom the question, but I really need it today. "Can... Can I wear pants, please?"

Mom's silence pierces my heart. I wonder what her expression is, but at the same time, I can't get myself to look at her. I wouldn't be able to face her if she's mad. "No, you're going to wear a dress, just like you do every day."

I can't do this anymore. I can't wear a dress today, I just can't. It's so painful and tiring and I don't want to feel the spiders climb all over me again. "Mom, please?"

"Gracie." Her saying that horrifying name makes me want to vomit even more. "I know you're probably still thinking about your father and what he wanted you to be, but you don't need to be that person. You are safe to be yourself."

"*I* want to wear pants."

"Honey, you've been brainwashed. I know you're confused and that makes things really hard right now, but it's okay. You're safe. You can be a girl."

"I don't want to be a girl. I want to be a boy."

"You are a girl."

"But Mom, aren't I perfect the way I am?" That's what she's always told me. That she loves me to the moon and back and that I'm her perfect little angel. "Because the way I am is a boy. Aren't I perfect the way I am?"

"But this isn't who you are, Gracie."

So... so I'm not perfect the way I am?

Am I not her little angel either?

"You're just confused. God made you a girl, and through that and Him, you are perfect."

"No, God made me the way I am, and I am a boy. I'm just a boy in a girl's body. That's what God made me as."

"Honey, just listen to what I'm saying. I know what's best for you, and you know I'm just doing this to help you get healthy."

"No! You need to listen to me! I feel so itchy and uncomfortable and like my body is eating itself from the outside and it's starting to get inside. I'm a boy. I need to be a boy!"

"Honey, don't think like that. That kind of thinking is the easy way out. I know temptation is hard and that your father implanted that thinking so far into your head, but that's how you go down Satan's path. Don't listen to Satan, Gracie. Listen to God. And listen to me—I'm doing what God would do, what Jesus would do, and He would want you to repent and get some help."

"I'm not wearing a dress! You can't make me!"

"Grace, you are going to wear a dress. It's only going to help you in the long run, I promise!"

I try to run away, but Mom grabs me by the collar and starts undressing me. I want to kick and scream, but I can't do that to my own mother. That... and I don't really have the energy to fight.

I try to speak and tell her to stop, but as she throws the dress on me, all I can do is cry as the invisible spiders start crawling all over my skin, from my legs all the way to my neck. This time, though, I can feel their fangs biting into me, and it's like they're injecting their venom into my body, and that venom starts spreading from my arms to my legs to my stomach, where it makes me feel queasy and it seems to turn on itself. It finds its way to my heart, where it feels so weak, and my heart stumbles and falls out of me. And I swear it keeps falling and falling and falling below me. I didn't know that it could fall that far.

"Stop crying, Gracie, it's just a dress."

Suddenly, the venom causes my body to become stiff and out of my control. I can barely think. I feel so light-headed and like I'm swaying back and forth, like I'm on a boat. I'm surprised I'm still standing. But I can't really get myself to move or do anything.

I'm trapped in my own body.

I want to scream at my mom, I want to yell to Mom that it all hurts and I want to get out of this dumb dress and that I feel so ill right now, to the point where I don't know if I can get better. How can I feel like this and somehow get better?! The health I used to have and the bliss of everything before my body started morphing into this monster seems like a dream now. I feel like I can't really remember it, and even though I know I was happy then, I don't know if I can ever return to it.

"Gracie, stop. It's just a damn dress. Stop being so immature about it. Now, let's get in the car."

I somehow walk myself to the car and get in my seat, deep down knowing I'm on auto-pilot. I'm not really thinking or aware of what I'm doing. The spiders and the venom and how I'm just dying take all of my focus.

The car starts up, and it's only after our home leaves our view that Mom starts talking. "Now, Gracie, I know this is hard for you, but I think the best thing for you right now is to go somewhere where you can get some professional help. What your father did to you is sad and absolutely disgusting, and I know that it affects you even though he's gone. And I know you're not going to be happy with me about this, but... but I just want to do what's best for you. I want you to get better."

I start feeling like I'm going to pass out or die as I sit in the car.

"So... we are driving to this camp. You're going to go there for a while and they'll get you right back on your feet again and make you the same old Gracie. You'll make all sorts of friends and you're gonna talk with some nice therapists."

Out of the corner of my eye, I notice some bags on the far seat. It takes me a second to really process what's going on.

"Now, they've dealt with a lot of kids like you. Kids who think they're the other gender because they've been brainwashed by the homosexual agenda. They know exactly how to cure your confusion and make sure you get back on the right path of being one of God's disciples."

No.

No. No. No! No!

Anywhere but there! I'm gonna die there!

Please no! Please!

I don't want it to end like this!

Dad...

Dad... where are you? Please help me.

I need you.

Chapter 10

Dick

 feel so terrible.

I'm the worst father in the world.

I left my kid.

I shouldn't have left my kid, especially with the way Carol was acting. My sweet Robin doesn't deserve to be stuck the way he is with her being like that. I wanted to stay—I was going to stay in that moment—but then she started throwing things at me and things kicked in and I went into fight or flight, and I was dumb and chose flight.

I'm so sorry, Robin.

I didn't mean to do that to you. I didn't mean to say your name or call you a boy; it slipped out and I know I screwed you over because of it. I really was trying to hold my tongue the best I could and speak up for you at the same time. I guess... I guess my best wasn't good enough.

When I feel the fear is far away enough, I finally stop driving and just sit there and cry. I kind of lose track of time, but at least the sun hasn't risen when I grow too tired to continue. Polaris is still high in the sky. Looking at it reminds me of Robin.

Robin... please know that I'm so sorry. I never wanted to put you in that situation. I'm so sorry. I couldn't even fathom that it would all turn out like this. I hope you're okay.

Eventually, I'm able to drag myself around and find a hotel. Thankfully, they have some rooms available, so I check in and carry nothing but the t-shirt, jacket, and jeans on my body and a phone charger up to my room.

The first thing I do is plug in my phone and fall onto the bed. I just don't know what to do. I want to go to sleep so I can start anew, but it's not like I'm going to wake up back home with my wife next to me and Robin down the hall.

Life is never going to be the same.

I might not ever see Robin again.

My phone buzzes, and even though I don't want to entertain more pain for the night, I still pick it up. Maybe there'll be some good news about my son.

Instead it's a text from Carol's mother.

How dare you hurt my grandbaby! How dare you lie to my sweet angel of a daughter! You're a disgusting and pathetic excuse of a man. You are nothing short of a predator sent from Satan himself. I can't wait for the day you rot in hell.

Predator?

I'm... I'm not a predator. I can't be a predator! I can't become the thing that hurt me. I promised myself that I would never become that!

What if I am?

No... No I'm not. I've never hurt Robin that way. I know that for a fact.

But why would she call me that?

My phone buzzes again as I get another notification, this time from one of Carol's sisters.

You are a terrible man! I knew from the beginning that you were fake! I tried to warn her about you and how you weren't the one, and after all these years, I'm glad we're finding out that I was right. I pray to God that you have a horrific death as soon as possible. You should be rid of this world for trying to make your daughter a transgender!

Transgender?

Wait... is that what Robin is? Transgender?

All of a sudden something doesn't sit right in my stomach. As more and more messages keep coming, I quickly search the word up on the internet. And what comes back are claims that gender ideology is pornographic and sexualizing children and letting pedophiles get away with their crimes. People even claim that the ideology is like drugs.

What... what did I just read?

My child is transgender, which I guess would arguably mean that they believe in gender ideology in some way. And Robin has no idea what sex is, let alone pornography.

I keep reading just a little more, finding declarations that becoming transgender is a sign of trauma and how identifying as trans and taking drugs to ruin your hormones is causing a decrease in mental health.

I can't get myself to believe all of that.

Robin was so sick and sad, and when I started calling him Robin, he was so happy. He even gained back some energy just at the mention of his name, or even just at the fact that I called him *son*.

But I don't want to hurt Robin. What if the article is right? What if he's just going to get worse the more we go on? I mean, an article on the negative impact of puberty-blocking drugs was written on it. There's even a study and it says that thirty-four percent of kids experienced a decline in their mental health!

And that thirty-seven percent experienced no change at all.

And that twenty-nine percent experienced improvements.

So... it's more likely that your child could have no change in their mental health at all than having it get worse?

But then why does the story make it sound like your child's doomed?

It even says the results of the kid's mental health could result from other things in their life at the end of the article!

This can't be real. This can't be legit.

But this is the news that is always on at Gramma's. It's what Carol always reads and watches. They're a respectable news source. At least, that's what I've been told by everyone in my life.

But then again, according to that news, I'm a predator and a child abuser and should be put on a sex-offender list because I simply call my son a boy and by the name Robin.

That's why they were calling me a predator.

I guess we have a different definition of that word then.

More and more of those texts keep coming and coming. It seems like they're going to last all night. They call me all the names in the book, and every time they call me a predator, it hurts me more and more. I know it's not the truth, but a part of me wonders if it is. The sheer amount of people telling me I am one makes me think that maybe I'm delusional or something. It hurts when people you considered your brothers and sisters when you had no one else accuse you of a crime that you had been a victim of as a child, a crime that had made you promise as a child that you would never do wrong to anyone.

I feel like someone has grabbed my heart and torn it out of my body. The simple idea of disappointing the child I was made me want to sink into the ground and never come back up. I failed little me.

It's hard to remind myself that they are just spitting out the lies they have been fed. Even though I know it's all fake, it all feels so real. Or like it's supposed to be real, so I should believe it's real.

Maybe I did fail myself. What should I do if that's the truth?

Well... I guess I only have failed part of my promise to little Richard.

I failed to not be a predator. I guess.

But I haven't failed Robin. At least, I haven't failed him enough yet.

I need to learn more for him. What else is out there that can help him? Who are other people like him? Because it sounds like he's not alone.

I may cry myself to sleep tonight, but not before I learn what a real trans person is.

Chapter 11

Dick

It's been a week since I was driven out of our home. And every day just gets worse and worse. Carol never called the cops nor texted me, but her family keeps harping on about how I'm a pedophile and a vile person, and they have made it explicitly clear now they are no longer my family.

With so much time and nothing to do, I try to make the best of it and learn more for Robin. Did you know that once you're old enough, you can get hormones for the gender you identify as? (Identify/identity is one of the words I learned. It's the gender that someone presents as, like how Robin presents as a boy and uses he/him pronouns). I never realized that was something trans people can get. There are some places that do it, like Canada. And it turns out that there are lots of people like Robin.

Some identify as girls, some identify as boys like him, and there are some people who identify as neither, who are called non-binary, and they can go by a whole range of other pronouns (I don't think I learned them all).

Learning for my child's sake is the only bit of joy I ever feel, though.

For a week, I've just been sitting in a hotel room, researching all I can about transgender people, going to work, and that's about it. It's hard to do anything else when your whole life has been screwed over in a night and you're constantly being made to believe that you've hurt your child. I haven't looked into finding a new place for myself. I've been too busy thinking about Robin and how much I betrayed my son.

I hope he's not mad at me.

I hope he can forgive me.

I understand if he never wants to, though.

On my one day off of the week, I just lay in bed, staring off. I hope Robin's okay. I hope he hasn't tried to hurt himself or has thoughts on ending his life. That's the last thing I want my kid to go through. It's not pleasant.

With thoughts of Robin, I pick up my phone. I wonder if I could get a glimpse on how he's doing. It takes a bit of hyping myself up to even be able to open the app that can lead me to my answers, but after a moment, I open Carol's social media page.

The only problem is she blocked me. I can't see a thing.

How the hell am I going to find out if my kid's okay?

I don't have anyone to talk to or anyone that can look at Carol's page for me so I can see if my poor son is okay.

It's not like I can make a new account and look through that. At least... not on my phone.

But if I went to the library and made one on the computer, I might be able to.

I hastily throw on some pants and my military green jacket before running down the stairs and to the library. This has to work! If this doesn't work, I don't know what I'm going to do—I don't know how I'm going to check on Robin.

Even though the library is a good ways away from where I'm staying, I make it there in ten minutes. Upon arriving, I have to wait for an open computer, but that only takes about five minutes. When a teenager leaves the computer she's on, I jump for the seat. I've never gotten on social media so fast. The last time I had done so was probably when I was a kid.

It thankfully doesn't take me long to make an account, and quickly I put in my wife's username. It takes forever to load, and even though I know the computer's working as fast as it can, it feels like it's purposely trying to stop me. Honestly, the whole world feels like it's trying to stop me.

Thankfully, her page loads successfully, showing all her posts, but the most recent one catches my eye.

It's a photo of Robin from Christmas, forcing that unfortunate smile and having to stand in that poor dress. Fear creeps all over my body, and for a second I'm too scared to read what the caption says. It takes me a moment to gather myself and read it.

I just recently found out that my poor little Gracie has been groomed and fallen victim to the homosexual agenda. I can't believe my own baby has become victim to all this. The radical left is hurting our children, but I'm making sure that my little Gracie is going to be okay, I'm going to make sure that she gets help. Please keep her in your thoughts and prayers as I drive her to her first day at Camp Magdalene.

The way she phrases it all makes me feel queasy. It sounds like she's doing the right thing, like she's the hero. If I didn't know anything that's going on, if I didn't know how my poor son's feeling and learned for him, I think I would've fallen for it too. I would've just trusted Carol and that she knew what she was doing, and how whatever Robin was going through was beyond my grasp because "she was becoming a woman."

Thinking about it, Carol probably thinks she is doing the right thing and that she is protecting her child. But... but what feels protective about sending your clearly sick child to a camp? Why won't you listen to your child about what's going on in their body? Because you sure aren't in it, so you don't know what's going on.

Never mind that, right now I need to focus on Robin. Camp Magdalene, let's look that up. I type it in the search engine as fast as I can. I quickly click on their website and look over their "about page" to get an idea of what they are like. I don't have high hopes for them.

And looking at them being all about how the left is too woke and how their goal is to fix the unnatural tendencies of kids who have fallen for the indoctrination of the radical left and to bring them back to Christ and family values, all hope diminishes in that moment.

I remember when family values meant something. At least, I knew it was supposed to mean something. I knew it was supposed to mean good things and looking out for your kid and making sure they're raised right and have their innocence by having access to age-appropriate things.

But I think it's safe to say that Robin sadly has lost his innocence because of these so-called family values. The family values that my wife believes in and told me to trust because surely those values would protect my kid and not harm him. Not make him so stressed and uncomfortable that he gets terribly physically ill.

It feels like my whole life is a lie. All those sweets are beginning to taste sour in my mouth. I can't believe I just took it at face value and didn't think twice, didn't look into it. I feel guilty that I was someone that stood for those things. How many people have I hurt because I was part of that group and insisted on those things?

Even though I've done wrong in the past, now is the time to change and start being who I am. And right now, that's getting Robin out.

I write down the address and bolt out of the library. I get in my truck, make sure I look well-dressed and groomed, and then book it for the camp. It's a bit out of the way, but what's important is getting there and getting him out.

It takes longer than I would've liked, but I eventually arrive at the place. I try my best to think of it positively. It gives me time to think about how I'm going to get Robin out and what story I'm going to give. Hopefully it'll work and I haven't been blacklisted yet by Carol. And if I am, then I'll figure out another way to get him out.

I park my car and start heading for the front office, trying my best to not look like I'm in a hurry. If I look like I'm in a hurry, then I'll look like I'm going to break someone out. I want to look like I'm one of them, and that requires me to be cleanly, calm, and act like they're doing God's work.

When I open the door, I hear a bell chime above my head. There's a lady at the desk, and when the bell rings, her attention turns to me. A friendly smile spreads across her face. "Good afternoon, sir."

"Yeah, good afternoon to you, too." Keep calm, Richard. Stay cool for Robin. Looking around, there's a lot of things hung up in the front office. There's an embroidery of the ten commandments, and a painting of Jesus reading to children. After seeing things like these all my life and feeling indifferent to it, it's so odd to feel unease at the sight of them. I feel like some of the children in the painting are staring into my soul, as if daring me to disobey what they believe in.

"Is there anything I can help you with?"

"Yes. I'm here to pick up my daughter. I believe that she was dropped off here earlier."

"Unfortunately, our policy is that we are not allowed to release any of the girls until they have shown clear indications that they are on the path of discipleship for Jesus. And even then, at that point, they would need to spend a few years in a boarding school so we can make sure to re-state that they are made to love God and show His love to the world."

Oh crap, how am I gonna get my little Robin out? "Oh, you don't understand. My wife, she... she unfortunately has gotten possessed by the devil. She's been having fits and her moods have been changing violently, and it seems that this time she took our daughter away from the hospital that was giving her care and brought her here."

"Do you know why your wife brought her here?" Her posture shifts a little bit. She seems nervous from the story.

"I don't. That's the problem with these fits. They come out of nowhere and she does drastic things with no thought or reason. She even lashed out at her own mother, who she loves very much."

"I see."

"Can you at least just please take a look at my daughter? One look at her and you can tell that she needs to be in a hospital, if you don't believe me."

The lady's quiet. She thinks to herself for a moment. "Let me go talk to management. I'm sorry that happened. What is your daughter's name?"

"Grace Wright. Her mother is Carol Wright."

"I see. That's so odd. She seemed rather normal."

"That sounds about right. At first glance, she's always normal to strangers. That's why it's been rather hard on us. People tend to believe her despite how outlandish her story is. It's brought a great deal of pain on us, and even though we're getting her help—and praying constantly—it hasn't been enough yet."

"I'm so sorry. Let me go talk to my boss and we'll get something figured out."

The lady rushes out, and I hope that my story is believable enough for her to let me get Robin back.

I end up having to wait quite a while. An hour has passed when someone comes back, and it's the lady with a few bags. Then little Robin, wrapped up in a blanket and accompanied by another lady. I'm so happy and beyond relieved to see my son. I can feel my body loosen, but not completely. I know we still aren't quite out of the woods yet.

"If you don't mind, can we see your license? Just to confirm you are her father."

"Yes, of course. What are you checking it with?" I start pulling my license out of my wallet, trying to be calm and not sweat. What can they be checking it against? Is it going to be something they can prove wrong?

"Her birth certificate."

That seems rather harmless. I hand her my license, and she quickly pulls something up on her computer.

I look over at Robin and smile at him. He doesn't seem very present, though. He looks sleepy and like he's about to fall down. Seeing him like this makes me feel so terrible. How could the world let him get to this point and do nothing about it? How could they not listen to my kid? How could they have not done the right thing and helped him?

I get down a little bit so I'm eye-level with Robin. "Don't worry, sweetie. Daddy's gonna get you back home."

There's no response from Robin. That scares me a bit. I hope he's going to be alright.

"Richard Wright?"

"Yes?"

"It seems like everything checks out. And for your information, she's thrown up three times since this morning."

"Oh, thank you so much for telling me that. I'll make sure the doctor knows when we get back. So sorry about the whole ordeal."

"It's alright. Usually when this happens, the parents regret dropping the kid off or there's a disagreement between the two parents, one of them usually being one of those liberals."

"That's absolutely terrible. I don't understand why any parent would stray from good old family values. It's disgusting." It feels revolting saying that, especially in front of Robin, but oddly enough, it's for Robin. "Well, thank you for doing what you can. I greatly appreciate it. Now, Gracie, let's get on going." Gently, I pick him up. Even though he doesn't move his arms, his head clings to my shoulder and wraps around my neck a bit, as if it's him holding onto me. After a second I can feel his tears drop onto me, which makes me want to cry, but I have to be strong for a few minutes longer. I just need to focus on how it's so good to have him in my arms again.

"Do you want help with the bags?" the lady who had brought Robin asks.

"Yeah. Do you mind carrying both of them?" An eleven-year-old Robin is a lot to carry. I doubt I can take his bags as well.

"Yes, of course. I'll follow you to your car."

With that, the three of us go to my truck outside. As I put Robin in the backseat and buckle him in, the lady puts the backpacks next to him. I thank her for it and make sure that she goes back inside the office before I hop into the driver's seat of the truck myself.

After I close the door, I look over at Robin, who's already drooping over. His head is leaning against the window. "Hey, buddy, it's alright. I'm here now. We're going to head over to my hotel room and I'm gonna get you better. Sound good?"

It takes him a minute, but he nods.

"Alright then. Rest up and don't worry about a thing. It's all gonna be fine," I make sure to tell him. Since I've eased him a bit, I figure it's time to get going. I start up the truck, pull out of the parking lot, and drive over to the hotel as I try to not cry too much.

Chapter 12

Robin

ad takes me to a hotel. When we get there, he lays me on one of the beds in the room and tells me to sleep, and that he's gonna quickly go to the store to grab some things for me. I'm so tired that I just nod my head and conk out.

When I wake up, Dad's already back. The bright, sun-lit room is now only lit by a lamp. Dad's laying on his bed, just staring at the ceiling. I'm surprised he isn't doing something else, like watching TV or maybe looking at something on his phone.

Since I feel well enough, I sit up. Dad notices that pretty quickly. "Oh, Robin, you're awake!"

"Yeah."

"Good. How're you feeling? Do you think you can walk a bit?"

I have to think for a minute. I feel a little light in the head, but not too much, I guess. It's been worse. "I think a bit."

"Perfect! I have a surprise for you. Come with me." Dad practically leaps off the bed and runs to the bathroom. What could he be so excited about?

I get up and slowly start walking over. It takes me a minute, but when I finally get there, Dad has a big smile on his face.

"Come in. You can't see it from out there."

I walk through the doorway, and he was right about me not being able to see. When I come in, I see some clothes sitting by the sink. There's a T-shirt with some cartoon characters, blue jeans, and a green hoodie.

And they're all my size.

I... Am I actually finally gonna get to dress like a boy? Be like a boy?

"I bought them for you," Dad tells me.

This... this can't be real. This is insane! Did Dad actually get these? I mean, they can't be for him, he's so much taller than me. And there's no one else with us, so they're clearly for me.

I actually get to finally wear pants. I can't believe I'm finally going to wear pants and not be stuck in a stupid dress.

"Now, I know you want to put these on right now, but you can't just yet."

Oh. I knew it was too good to be true. I probably have to wait for Mom to approve it because we're going to go talk with her.

"We're gonna wait because right now we're gonna cut your hair."

Wait... actually?

"And we all know that when you get a haircut, the clothes you wear get so itchy for days on end."

We're... we're going to cut my hair? And I get boy clothes?

I must be dreaming.

I... I actually get to be a boy.

I'm going to be a real boy.

"Now, come on, sit here." Dad pats on a chair he brought into the bathroom. I'm still a little bit in shock, so it takes me a second to sit down. As Dad pulls out a pair of scissors, I look at myself in the mirror. To think that all this hair is going to be gone! I can't wait to get rid of it. I won't need to comb it everyday, I won't have to deal with knots, and I won't need to straighten it. I also won't get hair in my mouth anymore. And most of all... I'll start looking how I want to look.

Dad gently grabs my shoulders and looks me in the eye through the mirror. "Alright. What do you want?"

I... I'm not sure. I never thought that far ahead. I never thought that I would get this far.

Dad can tell I'm struggling. "How about we start with just cutting it short? And then maybe you can figure out what you like from there."

I nod.

I watch as Dad opens the scissors and grabs a chunk of my hair. It's towards the front, and he very slowly starts bringing the scissors to the chunk. I think he's a little nervous about cutting it. I doubt it's because he doesn't want to do it. It's probably because he doesn't want to accidentally poke my eye out.

Slowly, the two blades start meeting each other in the middle, and I can feel the tension in my hair as it starts pressing against it and gradually separating it into two parts. The lower part starts falling down, some of it landing in my lap and some falling onto the ground. I watch as it falls, every being in my body absolutely overjoyed to see it go.

"Alright. First cut done," Dad says, more to himself than to me.

"Yeah. Now do more."

"Slow your horses, Robin. You're not the one with the scissors." Dad chuckles.

"And you're not the one who's been waiting for this your whole life. Just cut it!"

"I just don't want to mess it up. I know this is very important for you."

"As long as it's short, I really don't care." I look at Dad as I tell him that. I want him to know that I don't care. He's made this the best day of my life just by getting me those clothes—the haircut makes it one officially for the books.

Dad smiles. "Okay then."

Dad's cutting picks up a bit, and I get to sit and watch as my "perfect long hair" that went all the way down my back turns short. Yeah, it isn't the greatest, but I couldn't care less about that. Dad starts by cutting it to my shoulders, then goes a little higher, around my chin. When we get to that point, he then asks what I want. I don't want to stress him out with something complicated, so I just tell him that I want the sides and the back short, but to keep the front how it is.

It takes Dad a while, but he eventually gets the job done. Gazing into the mirror, I don't see dumb old Gracie anymore. I mean, I'm still in a dress, unfortunately, but I see *myself* in that mirror. And just seeing me, little ol' Robin Wright in that, is the most amazing thing that can ever happen to me. I feel so happy. It's weird because I feel so light. Like I'm on a trampoline and I'm so high up from bouncing. I thought I'd been happy before, but the joy I'm feeling in this moment feels so... so high and like I'm soaring through the sky.

"Well, it doesn't look too bad," Dad mutters, frowning a bit. "What do you think, Robin?"

"It's amazing!" I don't want to take my eyes off the mirror! That's me in there!

Hearing that makes Dad smile. And I watch it grow as he looks at me through the glass again. "I'm glad you like it. Now, you go take a shower. And when you're done, you can put your new clothes on, alright?"

"Got it, Dad! Now get out so I can take my shower!" I get off my chair and push him out. His laugh tells me he understands.

I have never been so excited to take a shower. Usually taking a shower is a little hard because I have to be naked and I don't like having to deal with my body, but this time there's something awesome waiting for me when I'm done. Like most showers, it sucks to have to see my body the way it is, but at least I have short hair now. It makes the shower a lot quicker.

When I get out, I dry myself off and hastily put my new clothes on. The t-shirt is nice. A lot more airy than I thought it would be. The jeans are next, and when I slip my legs down the pants and zip it up, it feels like all is right with the universe. It's so weird because this wave of relief just comes from above. It makes me feel so... relaxed. I feel like I can breathe. It's so crazy! And the best part is I don't have to "sit like a lady" and be all dainty because I'm not wearing a dress anymore; I got the jeans to cover me.

Last but not least, I throw the hoodie on. It's a lot softer than I'm expecting, and it feels so warm. I didn't realize how warm a hoodie could be. It's almost like having a blanket around you at all times. Almost.

I look into the mirror, so excited to see myself for the first time. Only problem is the mirror is pretty steamed up. I grab the towel and wipe the middle a bit. With the mirror clear, I finally get to look at myself.

My short hair is a curly mess and everywhere, especially since I took a shower. I kinda like it. The green hoodie is a little big, but not too big. You can see a bit of my t-shirt towards the top, which works pretty well with the hoodie now that I'm looking at it. And then there's the jeans, which helps me look just like a boy you would see walking down the street from school.

I look like an every-day boy.

And I have never been so elated.

Just seeing myself in the mirror, I feel so happy. That's me. That's a boy.

I swear I'm on clouds. I can jump and run and cartwheel with how much energy and joy I feel in this moment. It's been so long since I've had all this energy! Even though I know I'm on the ground and on Earth, I feel like I have a spirit inside me, and that spirit is just hooting and hollering as I fly freely in the sky that maybe is heaven. This is the most amazing thing that could've ever happened to me! I can't believe that it's finally happening for me!

My eyes start getting wet. Before the tears can fall down my face, I run out of the bathroom and straight to Dad's bed. He's just sitting there, so I tackle him down and give him the biggest hug in the whole world. It's all because of him that I get this.

My dad gave me the best day in my entire life.

Chapter 13

I have never seen my son happier.

That smile is so different now. It's from ear to ear, and for the first time, I notice that there's a little light to it. I don't think Robin's caught on to it, but every time I see him smile, it makes me smile. The pure joy he's feeling is just so contagious, and I find myself being happy just because he's so happy.

He's like a different person entirely. For the better, too.

He even was able to stomach some food this time. After hearing how many times he threw up at that disgusting camp, I was so grateful that he didn't vomit tonight. And it seems that whatever things he would've been forced to go through, he hadn't been subjected to yet. It seems I was able to come just in the nick of time.

Robin falls asleep pretty early. He sleeps in his new clothes, and as much as I wish he would've slept in his pajamas, I understand that all his old clothes probably will never be on his body ever again. I just can't imagine that sleeping in jeans is all that comfortable. It's not like he's going to part with them, though.

I'm just excited for tomorrow, when I can take him to get a whole new week's worth of clothes. It's going to be like watching a kid in a candy store. I can't wait to see what he comes up with; what he wants to try. Most of all, I'll get to see that amazing wonderful smile on his face again.

Turning my head and looking at my sleeping son is one of the most glorious things for me right now. Sure, he's asleep and drooling a bit on the pillow, and the haircut I gave him is an absolute hack job, but seeing him and knowing that he's overflowing with delight is the most marvelous thing I could witness and contribute to as a parent and as his father.

I'm glad that I could make sure one kid has a loving childhood and not one like mine.

No kid deserves to have to deal with parents like what I had. I don't remember much of it, but I remember enough to shudder. And then the foster homes were somehow worse. Sometimes I was lucky and didn't get hurt in some places, but instead I would witness other people getting hurt.

I can't believe that some people would hurt children. Especially their own. What has a child done to you? And no child is ever bad, you just need to get on their level and understand them. Getting in their mind and figuring out what's making them lash out or cry. It's not that hard.

No one ever did that with me. I would just get yelled at or hit or be called "troublesome" or "the problem child". Or my parents would drug me if I made a fuss.

And I can't believe that Carol is one of those parents.

I mean, she would never drug Robin. That's not what I mean. I mean... I don't understand how she decided that she was right and he was wrong and that he had to listen to her. She didn't even get on his level and ask why he was making a fuss. It immediately escalated to "mutilating his body and giving him drugs." No conversation, no learning, no nothing. That's not even what people like him do! I mean, I looked into it a bit; they do take a prescription that they might have to inject themselves with, but it's just hormones! The same hormones that I have. That's not really drugs; that's just natural chemicals in the body. It's nothing like heroin or cocaine. And the mutilation comment seems so out of left field. It's just surgeries, like ones that happen everyday. Carol doesn't make mean comments about how some celebrity she likes got stuff done on their butt, but the second it's about Robin wanting to change their gender, it's mutilation?

It just doesn't make sense. Especially because she's so sweet and kind, and rude remarks never go past her lips. It felt like a slap in the face that night. She turned into a whole different person. She even shoved me down the front porch, threw a bottle at my head. And she knows how painful that was for me in that moment. She knows that would trigger me.

I don't understand why the woman who loves me would put me through that.

Does... does she even love me?

No, Dick, that's a stupid thing to ask yourself. She's your wife! Of course she loves you. I mean, she wouldn't have married you if she didn't love you. She wouldn't have slept with you if she didn't love you. She wouldn't have had a kid with you if she didn't love you.

She loves me.

But... was she always the woman I loved?

I want to say yes, but something's caught in my throat. I wish I knew what was making me hesitate to answer that question. I mean, it would be crazy if she carried a whole facade throughout us dating and our marriage. But at the same time, there was a different Carol the night that she kicked me out. I can't deny that.

My phone buzzes against the nightstand. I'm a little surprised because I haven't heard anything on my phone for a few days. But it's probably some ex-relative that wants to tell me to f-off because of everything and how Carol's been painting the picture.

I pick it up, and to my surprise, it's a text from my wife.

The camp called me and said you picked up Gracie and that you told them I was crazy. Where are you? Where's Gracie? You better tell me right now!

Oh crap.

I look over at my son, sound asleep in his bed. Wearing his new jeans and t-shirt, his hair a bit in his eyes.

He was so happy today. To finally be himself. I will admit, deep down, I thought it was a little weird at first when he came with so many requests, but I went with it in hopes of trying to understand him and show some love to him. I didn't think it went this deep or would go this far. The Robin I saw today was the most active and delightful kid I have ever seen, and considering how sick he has been recently, it was so astounding to see that burst of energy. And to see him enjoy everything.

When he came out of the bathroom in his new clothes and gave me a hug is something that I can never forget. I have never felt him hug like that before. It was with all his little strength, and feeling that embrace from him made me feel so loved, and that I had done the right thing. He was even crying from how happy he was. Even though he didn't admit it, I noticed it. And even though he didn't notice, I cried a bit for him too.

What kind of father would I be to give him all that and the next day he has to go back to his mother? The mother who's going to strip it all away from him?

I can't do that to my kid.

My kid deserves so much better than that. He deserves to be happy and understood.

My phone buzzes again.

Richard, you better tell me right now!
Tell me where you're staying or I'm calling the cops and telling them you kidnapped my child!

I look at Robin again.

I... I love my wife. I don't want to anger her, and I don't like the idea of the police coming after me. A criminal record after all I've been through is the last thing I want. Little me would be disappointed in myself. If I bring Robin back to his Mom I wouldn't have to deal with any trouble like that.

But I also love my son. And little me would want me to do what's right and protect a kid, especially my son, at all costs.

I... I can't let my son go through what I had to go through.

That's the last thing I would want to happen.

What kind of father would I be if I didn't keep my son safe?

I'd be like my parents. And every adult that shut me up or hurt me.

Richard, if you don't tell me in the next minute, I am going to report you!

Robin... you are my son and my little baby boy. And I am going to do whatever it fucking takes to make sure that you are loved, that you are seen, and most of all that you can live your life.

I'm not going to let them fucking take you and screw you over like they did me.

I press the power button of my phone and shut it down. Completely. I'm not going to let them get to us.

I shove all my clothes into my bag as fast as I can and grab one of Robin's bags. It's purple, but purple is easier to work with than pink. Even though Robin doesn't have any comfortable clothes to pack, hopefully we can get some from a thrift store or somewhere. Something cheap that can serve us for wherever we're going. It doesn't have to last us long, and right now, we just need to focus on getting out of here.

When everything's in a bag, I shake Robin awake. It's hard because I know I have to be calm so he doesn't freak out, but I also need to get us out of here as soon as possible. I want to be out of here by the time the cops are driving down the street. "Hey, Robin. Wake up. We need to get going."

"Dad?" he sleepily moans. "What time is it?"

"Doesn't matter. Right now, we gotta get going, okay?"

"Why?"

"I'll explain later. Right now, we've got to get in the car. Follow me."

Once Robin's on his feet, I grab his hand and run out of the hotel room. I think we make it to the front desk in two minutes, which isn't as fast as I would have liked. I give the front lady the key card and check out. Once she gives the all clear, I grab Robin's hand again and book it for the truck. I don't know how long we can use it for, but I hope for a little bit. I buckle up Robin and throw the bags in the back-seat with him. Then I jump into the driver's seat and start the car. I have never sped out of a parking lot that fast before. As I get on the main road and turn to get on the path to Austin, I notice a cop car pulling up to the hotel in the distance.

It looks like we got out of there just in time.

Chapter 14

Dick

We barely make it to Austin by the time the truck runs out of gas. I'm able to park in a library's lot before it can't move anymore. Praise the Lord we were able to get this far. That being said, I doubt we can go any further with it. If the police came to the hotel, I imagine that Carol told them what my car looks like and who I am.

I hope they don't catch us. I don't want all of this to be in vain and for Robin to end up back where he started. I would never forgive myself if that happens. I just need to think of ways to give them less leads, or ways to make sure they can't find us.

As I look up at the stars, though not many are visible in town, I try to figure out what we're going to do. Where are we even going to go?

How are we going to make sure that the cops can't find us? How can we get to a place where it becomes a point of no return?

Or rather, where can we go that will help Robin? He needs help, and it seems the doctors around here are oblivious to what he actually needs, whether their oblivion is intentional or not. I have done a little bit of research on hormones and surgeries and stuff, but it sounds like there's only a few states that still do it. Even those might disappear soon, too. It feels like there's no place in America that can help Robin.

No place in America...

Maybe we need to leave the U.S.

If we leave, then the cops can't get us. Wherever we go, the U.S. and the government of wherever we end up would have to work together to turn us back in, and if the country we end up in is friendly to LGBTQ people, I doubt they would throw us back here because at this point we would be refugees. At least, Robin would. I don't know if I would really count, but what's most important is if Robin's safe.

Only problem is that I'm a wanted criminal and I don't have any source of identification for Robin, so getting past any sort of checkpoint is impossible. We can't fly somewhere, and I doubt we would be able to take a boat. Not one for the public, anyway. The only way we would be able to avoid any sort of checks is if we walk and avoid any border checkpoints in the distance.

Which I guess leaves us with Canada.

We need to run to Canada.

They would have what Robin needs. They would have doctors that would actually diagnose him with gender dysphoria and get him the things he needs, and they would know so much more compared to what I've learned. Not only that, but they also have free health care or something like that. And I can find some sort of job so I can support the two of us, and we can start life anew, and with the way things are turning, after all that I've read the past few days, I think Canada would protect us from the American government. Also, I've heard they're very nice over there.

But how are we going to get there? We shouldn't use the truck, and the police around here might know what Robin and I look like. Then again, Robin looks quite different now. Strangers might not be able to tell at first glance. But I'm still recognizable. I need to go to the store and buy some things to disguise myself. While I'm at it, I need to get a prepaid card so that the police can't track where I am through my purchases. God, I'm gonna have to think of every little thing to make sure that we don't get caught. Hopefully I'm remembering everything.

And as for transportation, we're not left with much. We can take a bus, but I doubt that would get us far enough fast enough. There's bound to be some sort of public transport that can get us at least out of here relatively quickly. I guess leaving the area would help us get a start on being ahead of the cops. While they're still looking in San Antonio and maybe Austin, we could already be on our way to Dallas.

Or we could take a train. Austin's bound to have a train station here. That would get us out of here pretty fast, and that would help us cover a lot of ground in a short amount of time. I just hope that there's a train going north that's leaving pretty soon.

I hear a yawn in the backseat, and I turn around to find my son waking up. His arms reach up to the sky as he stretches. After a moment, he opens his eyes. "Good morning, Dad."

"Good morning." I try my best to smile and not look stressed. The last thing I want Robin to be is scared of the situation, especially considering how sick he's been recently. Just a little bit of stress might make him sicker. I don't like the idea of keeping it a secret from him, but I just don't want him to get any worse than he is.

"Where are we?"

"We're in Austin right now."

"Cool." My son looks out the window with a sleepy grin, taking in the city for a moment. It's dark out, but it's slowly starting to come to life. You can see some people walking around to their places of work, ready to start their jobs. "Hey, Dad?"

"Yeah?"

"What was last night all about? When we had to leave our hotel room and stuff?"

Oh, what do I say? How do I hide this from Robin? "I've decided that we're going to go on a little adventure."

"An adventure? To where?" His voice was starting to teeter less, the idea stirring him up a bit.

"To Canada."

"Canada? Why Canada?"

"Because in Canada, you can be safe and sound. And once we're in Canada, we can look into other things for you. Like getting you boy hormones."

"Wait... I could get the hormones that boys have?" A more awake smile slowly spreads on his face. I can see it start to shine like heaven's clouds. "Does that mean that I could end up growing a beard? Or a mustache? Do I get big strong muscles too?" His excitement makes him jump out of his seat and lean towards the front.

"Maybe. Would you like that?"

"That would be awesome! It would be like I'm a real boy! Do you think my voice will drop too?"

"Probably." I'm not exactly sure what the hormone treatment does, but I doubt it would be much different than what puberty is like for someone who is born a boy.

Hearing that brings so much joy to my son, but it quickly passes. "Why do we have to go to Canada for it?"

"They unfortunately don't really have it in the U.S. I know it's going to be a long and tiring journey, but it's gonna be fine. We'll have fun while we're doing it—we'll make it an adventure."

"Like Robin Hood?"

"Like Robin Hood," I tell him. Seeing him grin at that makes me a little more comfortable about everything. If I can just distract him from the reality of everything, maybe it will all work out. At the end of the day, he's still a kid. He may not have all of his innocence anymore, but he still has some, and every kid deserves to have time to be a kid. "Now, grab your stuff. We're gonna head out."

As he does, he asks, "what are we gonna do? How are we gonna travel?"

"We'll take a bus or train. Now, come on." I don't want to really sit in one place for too long. Not around here.

We grab all of our stuff and leave the truck. Thankfully, I was smart enough to have hit an ATM on the way here, so I have untraceable cash, but not many places accept cash, so the first place we're gonna hit is whatever store that's open and sells prepaid cards at this time of morning.

I hold Robin's hand as we enter a store, trying to not make it too tight but also have it be firm. We walk towards the gift cards. Hopefully we have enough for the trip. Hoping is all we can really do. As I grab the card, Robin asks, "why are you grabbing a gift card?"

"It's a special kind of gift card. It will help us pay for things."

"Why can't you just use your credit card?"

"It's just easier to use this," I tell him. Hopefully he doesn't think too much about it.

Robin is definitely confused, but doesn't say anything else. Instead, he asks, "what are we going to get for breakfast?"

I haven't thought that far. What can we have for breakfast? Something that's a bit on the go. Maybe we can get some fast food. "What about some breakfast sandwiches? Or maybe some pancakes. That sound good?"

"Sounds yummy."

"Good." I'm glad that some simple things are enough to satisfy him.

Before we leave, I also grab a beanie and some glasses to help disguise myself a bit. It's not enough, for sure, but something is better than nothing.

We check out and pay for everything, and I purchase a local paper. It could be my only source of figuring out what's going on in the world, and possibly how far Carol will pursue us. With that, we head over to the train station.

I put the beanie and glasses on, making sure to stuff most, if not all, of my hair in the hat. Hopefully the lack of seeable hair throws people off and the glasses in some way mess some perceptions.

"Why are you wearing glasses?" Robin asks as we walk over to the station.

"Oh, it's just about time I got some, is all," I lie. "Can you please hold my hand?"

"Why?"

"I just want to make sure you're with me." I also want to make sure that no one can grab him away from me. It would be harder for them to do that if I have a hold on my son. Even though he rolls his eyes, he listens. He holds my hand the whole time.

I go up to one of the kiosks and start looking for trains that are leaving. There are a few, but the one that sticks out to me is Chicago. That's pretty far north, and it's only a little more than a day's travel. Once we're there, we can get a bit of a breather and figure out how exactly we'll get to Canada from there.

The tickets are pretty expensive. Though I'm having some concerns, I think we're going to have just enough to get us by. Thank God six-hundred dollars is going to be just enough for me and my child.

Now that we have our tickets, all we have to do is wait. We still have an hour or so to kill before we can board the train, so Robin and I walk over to the nearest fast food joint. Robin orders pancakes and I get a bunch of breakfast sandwiches for both my son and I. Most of them I plan to save for the train ride, so I put a good amount of them in Robin's bag.

As my boy happily eats his food, his legs kicking up and down —which does make me smile—I pull out the newspaper I got. It's nice to have something covering my face without looking extremely suspicious. I'm just a man who wants to look at the news.

"Hey, Dad?" Robin pipes up after a bite or two.

"Yeah?"

"I don't want to eat anymore. I feel like I'm gonna throw up."

"Okay then." Looking at the food he's eaten, I can't help but worry. It's not a lot. But I also don't want him to throw up. And it's not like he won't be able to have food for a while. "You can stop if you need to. We'll save it for later. Just put the lid on it and put it in your bag."

As my son does that, I put my attention back to the newspaper. Before I can even open it, though, the article on the front page pops up and slaps me. I don't know how I didn't notice it before.

Families Come First Act passed into law, a huge celebration for the country!

I remember that act. I remember hearing Carol's brothers-in-law talk about it so passionately, and thinking that I should vote in favor because family's should come first. I didn't realize at the time that it was targeting people like my son. Hearing that it passed into law gives me shivers.

Last night, the Families Come First Act was passed, causing huge celebration all around the country. With the passing of this law, facilities will be built for those who have been convicted or have been under suspicion of pedophilia. In these facilities, they will be put into correctional therapy in hopes that they will be cured of their perverted nature. All pedophiles and perverts will participate in the now federal program of these facilities, which will also include learning discipline through participating in public works projects, a carefully curated curriculum to help with reform, and required Bible school and lessons so they can learn the error of their ways and repent to God. The program is rigorous, and only those who have truly changed will be able to re-enter society, for those who are worried that pedophiles can just resume wandering the streets once they're done. It is safe to say that, finally, after all these years, families will be able to come first in this country.

It's honestly disgusting and ironic, considering the article below it.

On Sunday evening, two men were arrested for pedophilic activity. Upon receiving an anonymous tip, the police raided the apartment of Mr. Donaldson to find him committing homosexual offenses against another man. Thankfully, the police were able to put an end to such crimes. While it seems that no neighboring friends or families were harmed, the investigation is still ongoing. It is suspected that more people are involved in this disturbing operation.

"I just can't believe it," Mrs. Volton, 43, a neighbor to Donaldson, told us. "He was just like everyone else. It's so scary, thinking that there's a pedophile right within the grasp of my children. As a mother, it's one of my worst fears that something so terrible can happen to one of my babies."

"Currently, Mr. Donaldson and Mr. Flowers are detained. They are not going to be a problem for the public any longer," Sheriff Nottingham commented. "Hopefully, if the Families Come First Act passes, this can become a thing of the past. If that passes within the next few days, I'm going to make sure that these two perverts are going to be the first ones in one of the new federal correctional facilities. I'm going to make sure that they're made an example of and people don't become what they are."

Looking at the photo of Mr. Donaldson and Mr. Flowers, they both look a little older than me. And last I remember, pedophilia is sexually pursuing a child, not two consenting adults, which I'm assuming is the case if the other man was arrested.

I, of all people, should know what a pedophile is. I had to grow up around too many of them.

Chapter 15

Robin

I know Dad isn't telling the whole truth, which bothers me. I'm not a dumb little kid; I'm all grown up now. That being said, I'm not exactly sure what's going on. I mean, I know we're gonna go to Canada, and that's super exciting, but I don't get why Dad can't use his credit card, or why I haven't seen him use his phone. And how are we going to get in Canada without passports?

When Dad and I finish breakfast, we go to another store that's open. When we walk through the doors, Dad tells me, "now, the train ride is going to be pretty long, so I'll let you get something to entertain yourself."

"How long is the ride?"

"Twenty-eight hours."

"Twenty-eight? Well then, I'm gonna need a *lot* of things to do." That's more than a day.

Dad laughs at that, but I don't get why. Twenty-eight hours *is* a long time.

We stroll around for a little while. There are all sorts of things in the aisles, like plush animals and magazines and books and toys. The only problem is that I'm going to have to make whatever I choose last for twenty-eight hours. I don't know if any of these toys can do that.

As I round the corner, I stumble upon the books again. But this time, something green sticks out to me. I almost don't believe what I'm actually seeing, but after a moment, I realize that the most amazing thing in the world really is sitting on that shelf in front of me.

A copy of *The Merry Adventures of Robin Hood.*

I can't believe they actually have it.

"Oh my gosh, Dad, look!" I grab his arm and run straight for the book. I'm so happy that they have it! I can't wait to read it over and over and over again! It's like Christmas came early. I point at the book to make sure he knows very clearly which one it is, just in case there's any confusion. "Look, they have *The Merry Adventures of Robin Hood*! Can I *please* get it?" I make sure to puff out my lip so that he knows I really really *really* want it. "I left my copy at home, and I really want to read it. Please?"

Dad's a little torn at first, so I make my lip even puffier. I would love to have that book back in my arms again. Honestly, if we're going to Canada, I might not have a copy of *The Merry Adventures* for a long while, and that would be absolutely devastating.

But Dad finally says, "Okay."

"Yes! Thank you so much!" I give him the biggest hug in the world so he knows I really appreciate it. With that, I grab the book off the shelf. Just having it in my hands again feels electrifying. I can't wait to be galloping in Sherwood Forest again.

"And you can get one toy as well."

"I can get a toy, too? Thank you—you're the best dad in the whole world!" Now, I have an important decision to make. I dash straight back to the toy aisle. Whatever I choose now doesn't have to last twenty-eight hours.

I'm torn for a little while about what to get. I can get a dinosaur or army men, but that's not really something I feel would work well on a train. Also, I bet they would get old after a while. I've always wanted those, but I don't think that would be it. And as much as a football would be awesome to play with, there's not really space to throw it on a train.

Since those are out, there's only one other toy that can contend. And it's a toy that I've always wanted to play with. I would always see my cousins build whatever set they got, and as much as I always wanted to go and build with them, I wasn't really allowed to. But now, I can build my own.

"Dad, can I get the LEGO set?"

"Of course."

"Yes!" I get *The Merry Adventures and* a LEGO set? This is sick! Being a boy is awesome! I can't wait to build the LEGO, and then read after. This is going to be the best adventure yet! "I've always wanted to build one of these."

"They're very fun to build. Do you think maybe I can help you with it?"

Of course Dad would "want to help me." He really just wants to build the whole thing. I'll let him build some, but *only* some of it. "Maybe. I at least want to build most of it the first time."

"That's alright. If you need help, I can help you though."

"Dad, it's pictures. It's gonna be easy."

He puts his hands up in the air as if he's guilty of a crime. He sure is. The crime of not letting me do my own thing. "If you insist."

Oh, I do insist.

Since I have my two things, we go to the checkout and buy them. Then we make our way back to the train station, since it's almost time to leave Texas and begin our new "adventure."

Chapter 16

Robin

It's been a few hours since we got on the train and started moving on to Chicago. As the wilderness passes by our window, I continue reading *The Merry Adventures*. Even though I don't have a bookmark for where I was before, I know exactly where I had left off. I have read this thousands of times and I never get tired of it. It's awesome to read about Robin Hood stealing from the dumb old Bishop of Hereford so that Sir Richard can rightfully have his land back. I wish I can be like Robin Hood one day. Stealing from the dumb rich people and giving it to the poor. I honestly don't get why rich people need all that money. Some of them have billions! If I had billions of dollars, I wouldn't be able to spend it all, and then it would just sit in a bank account. What's the point of that? Especially when it can actually go to someone who needs it. At church, they're always talking about the impoverished kids in Africa, so why don't the rich people give all that money that's sitting in the bank to them?

As much as I want to read more, I kinda want to do something else. That, and I need to go to the bathroom. The only problem is I'm anxious to go. I've gone to the girl's restroom all my life, and as much as I would feel a lot more comfortable going to the girl's restroom, I'm a boy now, and I want to be treated and seen as a boy. I would feel safe going in the girl's but it would feel weird and not right. But what if I go into the boy's restroom and they can tell I'm different? Once I sit down and pee, they'll see I'm sitting on the seat and I'm doomed!

What if I just don't go? Then everything will be fine and I won't have to worry about this. But... at some point I might pee my pants.

"Dad..." I pipe up. I try to be loud enough for him to hear me but quiet enough for other people to not.

"Yeah, Robin?" Dad yawns.

"I need to go to the bathroom."

"Okay. It should be in the back of the car."

How can he be so calm about this? Then again, he hasn't had to deal with it before. I lean toward him and whisper in his ear, "but I'm scared to use the boy's bathroom."

Thankfully, that's enough to wake him up a bit and understand. "Do you want me to come with you?"

"Can you please?" I don't want anything to happen to me. And I also don't want to pee by myself.

"Yeah, kiddo. No need to worry."

I want to argue that there's plenty to worry about, but I know he's just trying to calm me down.

We get out of our seats and head to the restroom. It's not super far, but every step makes dread seep into my feet and race up my legs. What if some random guy notices how I pee? How is Dad going to protect me from that?

When we get to the small bathrooms, Dad pulls open the door to the men's restroom, and that's when I learn that the bathrooms on the train are just singular stalls. Inside them is a toilet and a sink, and some other weird thing on the wall, like any other bathroom.

"Oh." All the anxiety in my body melts into the floor, and I wish I could melt into the floor with it. I feel so bad for dragging Dad with me.

"It's okay," he assures me. "Now, go use the restroom."

I go in and close the door. I also, of course, lock it. I don't want anyone to walk in on me, even if Dad's probably just going to stay right out there.

I do my business, and of course nothing goes wrong and everything's completely fine. I know that in reality it couldn't have been that bad, but... but people are just so scary. It's crazy how invasive they can be, even if it's just about me going to the bathroom and which room I go to the bathroom in. Why do so many people lose it over something like that?

When we walk back to our seats, I ask Dad, "what's the weird white thing that was on the wall?"

"It's called a urinal. Men use it when they just need to pee."

I think that's a little weird. Why do they get a special thing for only peeing and girls don't?

***

"Hey, Dad, do you think you can teach me how to be a man?" I ask him as we're sitting in the cafe car of the train, building the new LEGO set.

"What do you mean?"

"I want to be a real man when I grow up. I want to do manly things. Can you teach me?"

"Of course."

"Can we start? Like right now?" I don't want to wait; I want to learn as much as I can.

"Well, there's not much that I can teach you now, we're on a train."

"Well, maybe tell me what things are manly things. We can start there," I plead. I want to know what it's like—I want to be a real man when I grow up. I want to be strong and tough.

Dad has to think for a minute. I guess there's a lot to being a man that I don't know about. "Well, when you're a man, you've got to be strong and do a lot of strong things."

"Like what?" I'm gonna do all of the strong things. I'm gonna be so strong. I'm gonna be the strongest man alive.

"Well, you've got to carry a lot of things. Sometimes it's small, like groceries, and other times, it's big like a couch, or heavy like a kid." Dad chuckles a bit as he gives me a light punch in the shoulder.

"Come on, I'm not that heavy. I bet a couch is heavier than me."

"Oh, it is."

"But, there's gotta be more to being a man than being strong, right?" Like, yeah, guys are strong, but that's not *all* they're about. I know they also do stuff that's both stupid and fun, and once you're old enough, you drink beer with your buds.

"Yeah, of course! There's... Men know very well how to survive in the wilderness."

"Are you saying that just because *you* like nature?" Now it seems like Dad's just trying to get me into things he likes.

Dad gestures to himself. "Well, I am a man... so I think that's a man thing."

Whatever.

"Besides, I know plenty of other guys that love nature. I mean, you love it, and you're a man."

I'm a boy, but I guess one day I'll grow up to be a man. "Is there any stuff about nature that you haven't taught me yet?"

"I need to teach you how to start a fire. And how to make a shelter if you don't have anything."

"How do you make a shelter if you don't have a tent or something?"

"It involves a lot of sticks, leaves, and sometimes moss."

That sounds disgusting... I love it. "That sounds awesome! Do you think we can do it on our adventure?"

"Maybe."

Yes! I can't wait to build my own shelter. It's gonna look so awesome. "That's gonna be fun! But... why would someone need to make a shelter?"

"Well, sometimes people might get lost out in the wilderness, so they might have to make a shelter."

Getting lost in the middle of nowhere sounds scary. I don't want that to ever happen. "What should I do if I get lost?"

"Well, if you were with someone, stay where you are so they can trace their steps back to you. But, if you're on your own, the first thing you would do is find water, like a river or lake, and then follow it."

"Why should you follow it?"

"Because water always leads to civilization, and it's a strategy that's worked for thousands of years."

Thousands of years is a long time. It must be a really good strategy. "But what if you can't find any water?"

"Then... follow some power lines."

"Really, Dad? There's no power lines in the woods."

"There are some."

I doubt it. Power lines in nature sound like the dumbest thing ever. "But what if there are no power lines?" I can't believe I have to say "if."

"Then I guess you just have to follow the north star. You know where that is."

I do, and since the north star is always up in the sky and is always north, it's not like there would be anything after that.

"The north star is also something that people have used for centuries to navigate. You can always depend on it."

"I know, Dad." He always says that. The second he starts going about Polaris, he just goes on and on and on.

Even though I'm annoyed, he just laughs and smiles at me.

"Is there anything else on how to be a man? You've got to be strong, you've got to know how to survive in the woods, anything else?"

Dad puts his arm around me as he tries to think if there's anything more. I hope there's more. I mean, I would love to learn how to get strong and how to build shelters, but there's gotta be some other rule of manhood.

It takes him a while to come up with anything, but he finally tells me, "the most important thing about being a man is that since you're strong and know how to survive, you gotta protect the people you love."

"How do you do that?" Police are the ones that are supposed to protect you, so why is it one of the things that make you a man?

"Well, sometimes people in charge aren't always right, and even if they're big and scary and have more power than you do, if your wife or child is in danger, a real man will do what he can to make sure the people he loves are safe and don't get hurt." A little tear creeps into Dad's eye, yet he still smiles at me.

"What do you mean people in charge aren't always right?" The government always passes laws so we're safe and sound. A government would only want to do what's best for its people and what the people want. Governments were only bad in Robin Hood's time.

I wait for Dad to say something, and after a moment of silence, I'm nervous that he's gonna deem me too young to understand. "There are lots of people in this world who don't do the right thing. They just do what they want or what will benefit them. And then they persuade many people to think that it is the right thing to do. Sometimes using things that people look highly up to, but most of the time by flat out lying."

The government is lying? Just because it would benefit them? "How does it benefit them?"

"I'm not sure, but I think a lot of times it's control or money related."

So the government doesn't do what's right, they lie to everyone, and they do it for money? "Like how King Henry got mad at Robin Hood for stealing from the rich and giving to the poor? When King

Henry only helped himself, lied about Robin Hood being a terrible person, and all sorts of people would try to kill Robin just for the money?”

“Yeah... kinda like that.”

So... not much has really changed between Robin Hood's time and mine. I thought living hundreds of years later would make things much different, but it sounds like nothing's changed. How is that even possible? There's so much that's happened between the middle ages and today, and the King Henries of the world are still in power?

“Robin?”

I look over at Dad.

“There is one more thing about being a man, and it's one that so many people fail at.”

“What is it?” It sounds like the rule above all rules of manhood. Whatever this rule is, I have to follow it with all of my heart and soul. A part of me expects him to say “read your bible every day,” or, “pray every night.”

Instead, he tells me, “a real man—a *true* man—does what's right. No matter the consequences, he will defend the hurt and the broken and stand up to those in power. A man will protect the people he loves, and the people who need help.”

“Like Robin Hood?”

Dad grins. “Like Robin Hood.”

Robin Hood is a good man. I want to grow up to be just like him one day. I'll get big and strong, I'll learn how to survive anywhere and everywhere, I'll keep the people I love safe at all costs, and I'll do what's right and tell the government that they can stick it up their ass.

Don't tell Dad I said *ass*.

If I'm gonna be like Robin Hood though, I need to start now. “Dad, can we do push-ups here?”

"Why?"

"I need to start getting strong so I can be strong enough to protect everyone."

My father chuckles a bit at that. It bothers me because I'm being serious. I gotta start now if I'm gonna help anybody! "I think there's some space in the aisle, but if someone needs to pass by we have to stop, okay?"

"Okay!" I immediately go to the floor and start doing push-ups. After a moment, Dad joins me.

Chapter 17

Dick

It's getting late in the night as Robin and I sit in our seats. My son's slowly dozing off, even if it's not the most comfortable. It just matters if he gets sleep, mostly because I know I'm not going to get much, if any.

"Dad?"

"Yeah?"

"You know how you said that people in power lie so they get what they want?"

"Yeah."

"How do you know when they're lying?"

Oh. How can you tell? I'm just now figuring out how to discern it all, and I'm barely able to do that. I mean, I guess it really just comes down to how I first started understanding it. "You really just have to look at their actions. If they're hurting people, whether that's physically or emotionally, then they're not really good people, even if they claim it's for a good cause or reason."

"Why would it be a good thing to hurt people?"

I honestly don't really know. I just try to think of reasons why I found myself in that position. "Well... I think it happens because the people they hurt get labeled as bad people, whether or not they are that. So, in that sense, they lie so they can justify hurting those people."

"So, would the people who aren't lying not hurt people?"

To a point, I guess so. "It may not be perfect, but I think the good people would actually be trying to not hurt people, or at least not as many as the bad."

Robin nods as he yawns. I hope what I gave him is enough to see with clearer eyes. I'm scared that I might have misspoken or that he would mistake something I said for something else. I just want him to be smarter and better than I was. My son looks up at me. "How can I make sure to find out if people are lying or not?"

"Look into it yourself. Get other opinions, professional opinions, and ask questions." I think that's all I did. It sounds so simple, you would think everyone would do that.

"I'm glad you asked questions. But why don't most people?"

"They just do as they're told."

"So they just believe the lie?" my son asks. He looks so confused about how the world could possibly be like that. Disbelief in his eyes because he was taught that he had nothing to be afraid of, but in reality he had everything to be cautious of.

I just have to nod. Even though I want to lie and protect some bits of his innocence, I need to be honest to him about the bigger things that are beyond my control. I'm no better than the people in charge or the government if I just let him go about thinking everything's peachy.

"Did Mom believe the lies?"

I nod. I love my wife, and I only wish the best for her, but I don't know if there's a way to get her to understand the depths of it all. I couldn't even get her to try and learn for the sake of our son.

"And Gramma too? And everyone?"

"Pretty much."

"But why did you not believe the lies? Why did you ask questions?" my son asks nonchalantly, trying to make himself comfortable in his seat.

It's not his fault. He doesn't know how loaded that question is. He doesn't know how stressful our situation is, and I want to keep it that way. I don't want to put stress on him, that's the last thing he needs.

"Dad, can you please answer me?" He's getting a little pouty, even if his eyes are drooping. "I mean, everyone believed it. They just did as they were told. Mom, Gramma, my aunts and uncles and cousins, the neighbors. They all did as they were told. Why do they just listen to all that crap and you don't? Why are you the different one?"

I feel my body tense up at the mention of being the only one to rock the boat. It takes me a moment to assure myself I'm on the train with my son, and I hope that he's too tired to notice.

"Dad?" Robin asks again.

"I don't know, I just notice things," I lie.

He doesn't buy it. His brow furrows and he turns around and puts his focus on the dark night. I understand that he wants to know, but the problem is that he shouldn't have to deal with hearing the things I had to go through. I'm just doing it to look out for him, but he doesn't understand that I'm trying to protect him when my own parents didn't. I'm just letting him have the childhood I never got. A child shouldn't have to distrust every adult around them because of how many times they got hurt by them.

Robin curls up in his seat and continues to look at the stars and the dark trees, refusing to say a word to me till I say anything. The boy who got hurt by every adult around him, except one. Except me.

I hate how I already see too much of myself in my son. Because that means he's dealing with things he shouldn't have to deal with. How was I so blind to that?

I need to make sure he trusts me, because I needed someone I knew loved me and that I could trust, and I'm not about to let my son have the last bridge he has be burned.

"My..." Why is it so hard to get it out of my throat? They're just words! "My parents were addicts. They never took care of me, which is why I got taken away from them when I was four."

Robin turns his head to me, but I can't look him in the eye. It feels shameful to even speak about it. It's so weird, it's like there's a muzzle on my mouth, or something that's trying to prevent me from talking.

My vision starts getting blurry, and I can feel the weight of the tears I'm trying to keep in. All the while I'm still trying to pry that muzzle off. "And... and I was put in the foster system because surely my parents would get better, but they never did. And no one wanted to foster a boy who was going through withdrawals from his parents' actions 'because he might become an addict one day too!' And I had to be tossed from home to home like some kind of broken teddy bear, and it just gets worse and worse with every new home. I was screamed at, I was hit till I was purple—" I stop fighting for a second because I don't want the worst of it to come out in front of Robin. He doesn't need to know what happened behind that cursed closed door! The only problem with ending the fight is that I don't have any energy to continue it at that point. I can't hold in the weight anymore, and tears fall out of my eyes. "...Why would the government make me go through all that as a kid, and then ditch me on my eighteenth birthday and throw me onto the streets?"

Oh, I'm such a terrible parent. I just dumped almost my entire life to my kid all in one minute. That's way too much. Why did I keep going? I should've just stopped after my parents.

Robin's quiet too, and that's when I know I screwed up. He doesn't know what to think of me now. I'm not this perfect father he thought I was. I'm not this man that knows how to do everything and knows right from wrong. Hell, my whole life's been flipped over because I've learned that what I was told was right was wrong. I want my son to look up to me, but now that he knows that I'm broken and have been messed up ten times over, he won't see me as that fatherly role model that I used to be in his mind.

"Dad?" Robin finally speaks up. I'm nervous where this is going to go.

"Yeah?"

Robin looks at me, and he doesn't say anything till I look at him. "You're the strongest guy in the whole world."

That makes me cry a little harder. I don't know why, but all of a sudden I feel a lot lighter hearing my son say that to me. It feels like he somehow pulled a weight off my chest that I didn't even know was there. I feel like I can breathe a lot more.

"Is that why you would always lie about your parents?" I know he meant when people asked. He was never told about them, but he always knew I was being dishonest about it all.

"I don't like talking about them. And your mother's family would not like me if they knew."

"But that's not who you are. That's just your parents. Your parents don't make you who you are."

It's odd to hear that kind of wisdom from my child. It's also odd that just about all the adults in my life couldn't come to that conclusion yet here is my eleven-year-old son knowing better than all of them.

Robin's lucky to still have some of that innocence, especially for this long.

"I mean... look at King Richard. His dad, King Henry, *hated* Robin Hood. And King John, who came after Richard, hated Robin, too. But Richard didn't hate Robin. He wasn't like his father, or his brother. He knew that Robin Hood was doing the right thing, and he met him and respected him and gave him his reward for being a good person all this time. Who cares if you're not like them. You're doing the right thing, like Richard."

I know that's his wonderful adorable way of telling me to not listen to what everyone else says. To do the right thing and what I need to do, and probably to "use the power of my kingly speech to profess to all the land" or whatever King Richard does in that book.

Those... Those words hit a lot harder than I thought they would.

"And..." My son smirks from ear to ear. "Like King Richard, you got to meet a pretty awesome Robin Hood."

"Oh, Robin." I can't help but chuckle. "You're named after Robin Williams, remember?"

He's not happy with that. As he rolls his eyes, I laugh. Something about him being moody like that just makes things feel a little bit lighter. Like we're just a normal father and son aboard the train.

"I love you, Robin. And I'm sorry I didn't tell you those things. It's... it's just that those things are very personal for me. I haven't told anyone but your mother about it." And even then, the one person I trusted it with still found a way to hurt me like everyone else did. "I just want to protect you and keep you safe."

Robin shivers at that sentence. "That's what Mom would say."

"But I also want you to be happy. Because I know you being happy also keeps you safe." I look at my son's face, and for the first time in eleven years, I notice something. I always thought Robin looked like his mother, because he always had long hair and looked so beautiful. But now there isn't a trace of his mother anywhere. Instead, looking at him is like looking in a mirror that somehow takes me back decades ago. "Robin, I want you to know that you are nothing like your mother."

"Because just like I told you, your parents don't define who you are?" Robin's eyes seem to favor the back of his head again.

That wasn't where I was going, though. I was going to say that he was too much like me. In mind and physicality. But what he said is probably better to tell him. I shouldn't project on my son. He is his own person. "Yeah. Don't let her, or me, define who you are."

"I won't."

"Good."

Together, we look at the stars in the window. Robin tries to name as many constellations as he can remember before he finally falls asleep.

Chapter 18

Robin

e arrive in Chicago in the afternoon. Stepping off the train, I'm surprised how cold it is. Thankfully, we aren't out in the cold for too long. We immediately go to the first library we can find.

Dad says I can look at the books or read *The Merry Adventures* while he has to go use a computer. I still think it's weird that he insists on using a computer, considering that I know he has a phone. Maybe it died. We don't really have a way of charging things. Either way, I have to spend some time by myself.

I find a nice beanbag chair and sit down and read. It's kinda fun to get swallowed up into the beanbag.

Robin Hood and his best friend and right-hand man, Little John, walk through the forests, along with their new friend, Arthur a

Bland. I can imagine the sunlight through the leaves of the trees as I walk with them, joining their merry adventures that I long for. We're all chatting and laughing, especially about Little John being afraid of the rain.

Then Robin Hood himself puts his hand up, hushing all three of us. "Heyday! Yon is a gaily feathered bird, I take my vow."

We all look over to where Robin Hood is pointing, finding a man strolling along, donned in all scarlet. Not just any scarlet though, the finest any of us have ever laid eyes on. This is a man of riches and luxury.

"Truly, his clothes have overmuch prettiness for my taste," Arthur complains. Even though I think the stranger in scarlet looks cool, people who dress like that tend to be so annoying and full of themselves. I don't understand why someone would dare walk around these parts wearing such lavish clothes.

"Methinks thou art right, friend Arthur," Little John agrees.

"Pah!" Robin Hood spits. I agree. Pah! "The sight of such a fellow doth put a nasty taste into my mouth! Look how he doth hold that fair flower betwixt his thumb and finger, as he would say, 'Good rose, I like thee not so ill but I can bear thy odor for a little while.' I take it ye are both wrong, and verily believe that were a furious mouse to run across his path, he would cry, 'La!' or 'Alack-a-day!' and fall straightway into a swoon. I wonder who he may be."

A door behind me opens and someone comes past me. It distracts me for a second, and then I get more distracted as I watch the girl walk over to one of the counters where the librarians usually are. Her hair is absolutely beautiful. It's in a bunch of braids. I thought I've always hated braids because I never liked them on me, but I guess they can be amazing.

The girl, who's definitely a high schooler, is wearing a red puffy bomber jacket. It looks so warm and bright. She also has a beanie that's the same color. Even though her hat and jacket look really warm, I can't help but think her black ripped jeans make her cold. She has a backpack slung over her shoulder, which is adorned with all sorts of pins and patches. Most of them are bands, I think.

"Hey, can I talk with Maya?" the girl asks one of the librarians. It takes a few minutes for Maya to come, but she eventually appears at the counter. At the sight of the girl, she sighs. She seems disappointed just by looking at her. The girl couldn't give a care about it, though. "Did you see the news last night?"

Maya nods. "Oh, I saw it alright."

"You know that now's the time if ever. Even though I should've left a long time ago."

"Scarlett, don't go sassing your parents! You know they are doing their best."

"I know, but come on! Everyone saw this coming from a mile. Anyone who has waited this long is screwed."

"Now, now, I'm sure *you* won't be screwed. You're too stubborn, after all." Maya gives her a look. "How much did your parents give you and how much do you need?"

"They only gave me fifty—"

"Fifty? You've got to be grateful for fifty!"

"—and I don't know how much I need, but I bet it's gonna be more than fifty."

"Do you have a plan?"

Scarlett sighs. "I don't have a plan—"

"You *don't* have a plan?" The way Maya says it scares me, even though I know she's saying it with love. I'm glad no one's talked to me like that or I would've felt very ashamed of every action I have committed in my life.

"No, I don't. Because people don't really plan for escaping their murder, it kinda just happens. That, and my passport still hasn't come. I can't wait for that anymore. I need to go now."

"You're not going to be able to get anywhere without a passport, and I ain't gonna let you get in that kind of trouble. That's how you're going to end up in one of those facilities and die."

"Better than just being picked up by the police one day and never seen again. I'd rather die fighting. So can you just give me the money and I'll figure it out?"

Maya says something, but I can't hear what it is. Then the girl's head turns, and not only do I see her face for the first time, but then I realize that both her and Maya are staring at me.

And all of a sudden, I'm very scared and embarrassed.

"Boy, get your butt over here right now!"

Even though I want to cry in fear, I do as I'm told. I try to get out of the beanbag, but end up struggling to get out. I'm only successful after falling back in a few times, and then stumbling out of it. Once I'm back on my feet, I run over to the counter because I can tell that if I don't get there as soon as possible, things aren't going to go well.

Maya looks me up and down, all with a glare that eats away at my confidence every second. "I haven't seen you here before. What are you doing here, especially since you're eavesdropping?"

I try to get my thoughts in order, but they all come out in a jumble. "I-I'm sorry I was just—I'm just here—I was reading and—"

She puts her hand up at me, and I know that's to tell me to shut up. "Where are you from? And you better tell the truth."

"I'm from Texas, ma'am." I try my best to be polite because I know I'm on trial.

Maya looks over at the girl, giving her that same look from before. "At least he's got some manners. It's nice to see a child knowing how to respect his elders." I can tell it's a jab towards the girl. "What book do you have? Is it from here?"

The idea of talking about Robin Hood helps me breathe a little. "No, it's my own copy. It's *The Merry Adventures of Robin Hood*. It's my favorite book. I love Robin Hood so much! He's awesome."

"*Merry Adventures of Robin Hood?* And how old are you?"

"I'm eleven, and I've read it so many times!"

"An eleven year old reading *Robin Hood?* Now I've seen everything." She chuckles to herself a bit. I know that not many kids read *The Merry Adventures*, but I don't think it's *that* crazy that I read it. "What's your name?"

"Robin."

"Well, there's my answer."

"As much as I want to be named after Robin Hood, Dad always says I'm named after Robin Williams." Even though he's not here, I know that if he was, he would interject with that, *like always.*

"Well, Robin, I'm gonna ask you now, why were you eavesdropping? If you were raised right, you should know that's rude."

"I'm sorry. I just thought that you looked really cool," I tell the girl. She's quite a bit taller than me, and when I look at her face, I notice that her skin is really beautiful. It's a dark shade, and there's not a pimple anywhere. She also has a few nose piercings; one on the right side of her nose and another between her two nostrils. "And I also wanted to say that your hair looks really beautiful."

It gets really quiet between the two of them as they share a look. I don't really understand what it means, and now I feel really embarrassed. My cheeks get really hot. I swear I'm by a fireplace with how warm I'm feeling.

"Robin!" Dad yells. Of course *now* he's off the computer, when I'm not just sitting in the beanbag and waiting for him to be done. He runs over to us, and I know that he's worried that I messed our whole plan up. "I'm so sorry, miss. Whatever happened, I'm sure there's a good explanation. If something's broken, we'll pay for it."

"Nothing's broken, sir."

"Is he in trouble?"

"No, he's fine." Her look says otherwise, but I don't think I'm in trouble anymore. I can tell Maya wants to make a comment, but she's holding it back.

"Alright then. We best be going." Dad reaches his hand out to me, which I know means that I have to grab his.

But before we could start walking, Maya's voice finds a way back. "Excuse me, sir, you look familiar."

"Oh, you probably saw me the other day when I came in," Dad lies.

And Maya sees right through it. "Oh no, I didn't. I know everyone that comes into this library, and I know that I haven't seen either of your two till today. And your boy says you're from Texas."

Oh crap. I didn't think saying that could get us caught.

She has to think for a minute before she realizes where she's seen Dad from. And when she does, her eyes widen. "You're that man from the news!"

"The weatherman?"

Oh, Dad, you are *so* dumb for trying to get out of this with a joke.

Maya's finger starts flying around. "You're that man who abducted his daughter and whose wife is absolutely hysterical on every news outlet she can get on! I mean, she's crazy with all that nonsense she's sputtering, but you're as crazy! Where's your daughter?"

"Are you going to call the cops?"

Scarlett and Maya share another look. I'm a little confused about what they're thinking. It's weird. I swear they're talking telepathically or something. "Where's your daughter? How about you answer that first. Because all I see with you is a boy who—" She stops mid-sentence. She takes a good look at me, then types something into the computer on the counter. After a minute, she looks at the screen, then looks at me. Looks at her screen, then looks at me. "Oh."

"Please don't call the cops," Dad pleads.

"Oh please. If I call the cops, I'm more likely to get shot than you. But you better give me a damn good reason why I shouldn't give them an anonymous tip."

Now Dad's put on trial, and I get anxious that we aren't going to be able to get further than the library parking lot. "My wife put him in one of those correction camps back home, and he got so sick just from being in her care, I had to get him away. I couldn't let him go through those so-called therapies or corrections or whatever they call it now."

Maya looks Dad up and down like she had done with me. She gets back on her computer and types something. Her silence is deafening to my ears, and I bet it is to Dad's too.

"Says here," Maya begins, "that you pulled your little Gracie Wright from Camp Magdalene, which is a correction camp that 'works to bring the light of Jesus back to the lost little lambs of the world.' I agree with you, that's a bullshit explanation, but that doesn't explain why everyone's calling you a predator and the warrant for your arrest, which is for kidnapping, child abuse, and molestation."

People are calling my father a predator? Like one of those adults that hurts kids really badly?

Dad's about to say something, but Maya's hand goes right back up and she looks straight at me. "Now, child, you better listen to me very carefully. I know your father is right next to you, but you are going to tell me the truth and nothing but the damn truth, alright?"

I nod.

"What's your name? And your full name."

I don't know what to say because I don't want to say that terrible girly name, but I need to be honest. Maybe I should tell all of it. Or most of it. "Technically it's Grace Anne Wright." Just saying that hurts my heart. "But I hate that name! I don't have a middle name yet, but I would rather be called Robin Wright."

"And are you a boy or a girl?"

I hate that question—that shouldn't even be a question! "Well, I *should* be a boy."

"That's enough from you. You"—she goes straight back to Dad —"according to your wife, you're planning to give your kid drugs and mutilate their body."

"That's not—"

"I'm not done yet, sir!" Her finger comes back out, and I can see Dad sink a bit. "Now, if I didn't know better, I would say that you're a terrible, disgusting man. Except I'm not some crazy woman from Texas. I'm from Chicago. And in my career I've seen a lot of kids like your son, so tell me the full truth right now. I know that we're in public and there are laws, but if I decide that you're being honest, I might let you go."

Dad seems a little lost for words. I hate that it takes him a moment to gather himself. I don't want us to be seen as suspicious. In a near whisper, Dad tells Maya, "This is my transgender son. My wife didn't approve of it and thought that I was brainwashing him. She called the police and said I did all those things so she could have her way and take him back and make him go through those dumb correction facilities. I know what she wanted was not right, so I took him away and ran... which, I guess, also technically isn't right."

Her face doesn't change one bit as he says that. She looks at me. "Anything you want to add?"

I'm scared that if I don't say the right things, everything will be over. "He's the best dad in the whole world. I'm so happy he took me away. I... I don't know if I would be alive right now if I was still at that camp." It's kinda scary to think about that. In another world, a world where Dad didn't rescue me, I might be dead.

Maya's quiet. She looks at the girl, then looks at us. "Have you two heard of the Families Come First Act?"

I haven't, but Dad nods. "Not really a fan of it."

"What kind of sane person is? I take it that you have some plan because of it?"

Dad looks around to see if anyone's nearby before whispering, "yes."

"Are you heading to Canada?"

Dad nods.

"Do you have passports? I doubt you do if your child looks different than the photo of him that's in everyone's hands."

"We don't, but we're going to cross the border. I found a spot that we can walk, a good distance from border patrol."

Maya looks over at Scarlett, who seems annoyed about the idea. They don't share any words. Maya gives her attention to us. "I won't tip off the police if you take this young girl with you," she says, motioning to Scarlett.

"We only have enough money for the two of us," Dad interjects.

"She's got her own money! I just want to make sure she's going with someone that at least has half a brain. It's more than what she's got."

"How much do you have?" Dad asks the girl.

"Fifty bucks."

"She's gonna need another hundred dollars where we're going."

Scarlett gives Maya a smirk. "I told you it wasn't enough."

Maya begrudgingly looks at us. "What's your plan, exactly?"

"Taking a train to a town in North Dakota and then walking to the border from there. There's very few towns in between and the walk can be done in a day."

Maya turns to Scarlett. "How do you feel about that?"

"I'm just surprised you're suggesting that I follow a white man."

"I don't like it either."

"But... I think it'll work out." A little smirk spreads on Scarlett's face. "Better than nothing, I guess."

"Okay then." Maya pulls out her purse and hands her a card. "Go to an ATM and pull out a hundred dollars and then come right back. You're gonna give me my card and Imma make sure that you only pulled out a hundred, got it?"

"Yes, Auntie Maya."

"And once you cross that border, you're gonna pay back that hundred or I'm gonna travel to another country just to whoop your ass. And you two—" Maya looks right at Dad and I. "Stay right where you are. You're not moving until you and Scarlett leave for Canada. Can't have you getting into more trouble."

Knowing it comes from a good place, that makes me smile.

Chapter 19

Robin

hen Scarlett comes back and makes sure that all is set with Maya, the three of us go over to a store so that we can get her one of those gift cards that works on everything. She is also a little skeptical of it, but Dad explains what it is to her. He says it's a gift card for a company that's responsible for so many credit cards, and because of that, they're able to produce the gift cards and have them work like credit cards, but it just has a limit.

Once we get her set up, we grab some food really quickly. It's a lot more than last time. We just about spend all our money, except the amount we need for our tickets. It kinda scares me a bit, but I trust that Dad knows what he's doing. We must almost be there if we're using the last of our money.

Once we have just about stuffed our bags to the brim with food (mostly my bag since I don't have a lot of clothes), we head for the station. Dad buys tickets for him and I, but Scarlett has to buy her own. She's barely old enough to order her own apparently, but since her sixteenth birthday was a few weeks ago, she's able to get through well enough.

Since we have to wait a bit for the train to be ready, we all sit down and wait. I want to play with my LEGO set again, but sitting in a chair isn't the greatest place to do that, and I don't feel like reading *The Merry Adventures* right now.

I look over at Scarlett, who's on her phone. I notice there's a bunch of patches on her jacket, similar to her backpack. Except there's one spot where you can tell there's a patch, but it's covered by black tape. I can't tell what kind of patch it is other than it being a rectangle shape.

"Why is that patch covered?" I ask her.

She doesn't hear what I say, but she knows I said something. "What?"

"Why is that one patch covered but the others aren't? What does it look like?"

She doesn't need to look to know which one it is. "I didn't have enough time to take it off before I left."

"Why did you need to take it off?"

Scarlett makes sure to check that no one else is listening. "It's the lesbian flag."

"What's a lesbian? And what does the flag look like?"

"Wow, they really don't talk about anything in Texas," Scarlett mutters to herself. "A lesbian is when a girl, like me, likes girls."

"Like, like-like?"

"Yeah."

"I didn't know that girls could fall in love with other girls."

"They can. And this"—she pulls something up on her phone and shows it to me—"is the lesbian flag."

The photo of the flag has five lines, the top two are a dark then light shade of orange and the bottom two are a pink that turns a little purple with the last line. The two groups are split by a white line in the middle.

The colors are so pretty. "Wow. It kinda reminds me of a sunset."

"A lot of people say that," Scarlett dismisses. She looks like she's going to go back on her phone, but she stops herself. She looks at me for a second before deciding to speak what's on her mind. "Do you know anything about the LGBTQ?"

"Is that a sandwich?"

Dad, who *apparently* is eavesdropping, chuckles at that.

"You're thinking of a BLT. And it's not a sandwich. It's an acronym for people like us."

"Like us?"

"People who... who don't really conform to what society wants us to be."

"What does it stand for?" I ask.

"It stands for Lesbian, Gay, Bisexual, Trans, Queer. There's more after, but it mostly gets shortened to those five."

"What do the other ones mean?"

"Gay is when boys like boys. Bisexual is when you like both boys and girls. Queer is sort of a weird term. It's a little old or offensive in some people's opinions, but others use it kinda like a label because they're not sure what they are yet, but they know they're not straight."

"What does straight mean? Is that another part of the LG...T...BQ?"

"LGBTQ, first of all. If I'm gonna teach you, I'm gonna teach you right," Scarlett corrects. "And straight isn't part of it. It's what society wants everyone to be. It's when a girl likes a boy, or a boy likes a girl."

I think I'm starting to understand it a bit. I turn to Dad. "So you're straight?"

"Yes."

It's starting to click a bit. "So, why does society want that? Why does everyone need to be straight?"

"Most people say it's against their religion, even though it actually kinda isn't."

"You're saying that Christians lie?" I mean, I can understand in a way why politicians lie and what they gain from their greed, but Christians? Christians are supposed to be nice and kind and follow the Ten Commandments. Aren't we supposed to try and be like Jesus? Jesus wouldn't lie. "Why would they lie about that? It's against the Bible to lie—it's a sin. "

"Oh it is, but you'd be surprised how much they lie. Considering how much they act like they don't."

A part of me feels hurt by that. I've grown up around many Christians, including Mom and Gramma. Just about everyone I know in my life is Christian. They're nice people. At least... they *were* nice. I kinda don't want to believe the hypocrisy, that the things I've been taught growing up weren't being followed by the people who were teaching me. But at the same time... that's what it always was. It was always "follow the

Ten Commandments" or "follow the word of God" until it was something they didn't like.

I look over at Dad again. "Did you know that Christians lie? Are they just like the government?"

"Look at the government," Scarlett speaks up. "It's most, if not all, Christians."

That doesn't seem right, but the more I think about it, the more I remember all the adults talking about governors or senators that are religious and part of the Church.

I still wait for Dad to say something. As I watch him, he seems to stare into the floor. "I mean... I guess I knew, but your mom always told me that I was confused, or that I just wasn't praying enough or believing hard enough."

"Why didn't you say something?" If he knew they were lying, why didn't he call them out? Or ask for the truth?

Dad doesn't have an answer for that. The way he frowns makes me feel bad for putting him on the spot. I didn't think that talking about this would make him sad.

"Did you ever go to church because you wanted to go and sit and listen to a sermon for eternity, or did you just go because Mom made you?" I ask. "Because I only went because Mom made me. And..." And honestly... I also went so she wouldn't get angry at me, or because by the time we got there I would go to Sunday school and be able to get away from her and be with my friends.

I never liked going to church, I just liked being able to get away from Mom and have some sort of independence. All while making her happy, too.

Dad has to think for a while to figure out the truth in himself. "I... I went for your mother. I went a lot as a kid, mostly against my will, but back then I was a very wild child. And then when I got dumped out, I didn't go for a while. I only started going back because your mother insisted."

"So you never liked going to church," I have to state for him.

It takes a minute for it to really sink into his head. "I guess I never did."

It's so weird. I don't think I ever realized how much power Mom had over the both of us. I always thought that they were both pretty equal on everything and that they agreed on everything, but deep down I knew that wasn't the case. Mom was always the one making the statements or giving out punishments, and Dad would try to weigh in, but Mom would shut him down because "she knew best" and "she knew me better since he was always at work."

It was never Mom and Dad on a subject. It was just Mom, and Dad was forced to follow along.

Dad's always forced to follow along.

I think we're both realizing that right now.

"Y'all are really messed up down there. Didn't think it was this bad," Scarlett comments.

"It wasn't that bad," Dad begins to defend.

"Says the man who ran away from it with his son. It was bad enough that you had to leave as soon as you could, and last I checked that's pretty bad."

"Well, you're doing it, too."

"But I recognize that the situation was screwed. You're in denial about it. Well, some of it. You at least had the balls to see what was going to come out of it if you stayed."

Dad doesn't say anything. He kinda just looks away. For a second I think he's going to nod off and finally sleep. He... He hasn't really slept this whole trip. I don't think I've seen him sleep at all. He's always been awake.

Scarlett doesn't notice or say anything. She goes back to her phone. Before I can ask Dad if he's okay, Scarlett brings me to her. She has a different image on her phone. "Look, this is the transgender flag."

"Wait... I have a flag?"

"Yeah. Everyone's got a flag, and you're no different."

I look at it, honestly a little ecstatic that I get one. There are five lines. The first one is blue, followed by pink, then it mirrors itself. A white line splits the two mirrored groups. It doesn't look as pretty as the lesbian flag in my opinion, but the fact that it's a flag that represents me —and that it still looks pretty awesome—is what makes it so amazing.

"Whatcha think?"

"I think it's great! Do you think I could get a patch of it one day?"

"Maybe. Once we get to Canada, though."

"Yeah, of course." Wearing it around now wouldn't be the greatest idea. If Scarlett's covering her flag, I can't imagine I would be able to proudly wear my own.

"Wanna see some other trans people?"

"You mean there are other people like me? Who want to be boys and became boys?"

"Yeah."

I didn't know that. I thought I was the only one. "I would love to!"

Scarlett has to search on her phone, but once it loads, she shows me all sorts of people that are just like me.

~157~

Chapter 20

Dick

It's been a long day. For Robin and I, it starts and ends on a train. It's been hard keeping him entertained and distracted, and on top of that, we seem to have picked up another kid. I wasn't expecting that to happen. At least she seems nice and genuine.

Night comes a lot quicker than I'm expecting, and thankfully Robin's out like a light. He falls asleep reading *The Merry Adventures*, of course. Once I'm sure he's sleeping, I gently pull the book away from him and put it in his bag.

With nothing to do, since I know I'm not going to be able to sleep again, I gaze out the window and just look at the stars a bit. It's easier to see them when we're traveling through some barren land. I can see Polaris shining. It's a lot further up in the sky than back in Texas. As if it's finally rising to its brilliant glory.

I hear something to my right and turn around, a little startled. It takes me a minute to process what happened, but I realize that Scarlett just dropped her phone. She slowly picks it up and then curls up in her seat. I expect her to close her eyes and try to fall asleep, but she doesn't. She just stares off into the floor.

"Scarlett," I speak up. "You should probably get some sleep."

"I'll be fine." She's quick to shove me off.

"Please. As someone who's not had much, get some."

"Why don't you sleep then? And I'll stay awake to make sure nothing bad happens. I know that's why you haven't been sleeping."

I'm in a bit of a shock. She's not wrong. Rather, she's dead accurate. "You're very perceptive for your age."

"I was taught to see the world for what it is, unlike you all down there living in some fucked up utopia."

She's not wrong about that either. "I can't get myself to sleep. Even if you're watching out for us, it's a bit different when it's your child's life at stake. That, and we barely know you. No offense."

She rolls her eyes, but she understands. I expect her to go back on her phone, but she doesn't. "I've seen your wife on the news."

"So I've heard."

She gives me a look. "Have you not seen the interviews? She's absolutely insane."

"I haven't had the time to. I've been too busy being on the run and making sure Robin's okay."

"Good for you, Dad of the year," she jokes. She goes to her phone and pulls something up on it. "You *have* to take a look at this. It's crazy."

She hands me her device; a video playing of a national news segment. One of the news anchors is talking, but I can't really catch what he says, as it quickly goes to a reporter out in the field. That field being home back in Texas. Carol's standing in front of our house, crying and weeping. I feel so terrible just looking at her. I never would wish upon her the pain that she's in now. I took our kid from her, and even if it's to protect our kid, that doesn't dismiss the fact that she is grieving.

"It's absolutely terrible." Her voice crackles through the phone's speaker.

"I can only imagine," the reporter replies. "To find out your husband is a pervert, only for him to steal your child from right under your nose is absolutely despicable."

"I'm so scared for my little girl. He talked about injecting drugs into her and making her go through horrible surgeries! This is why we need laws about this! We need to protect our little girls from people like him. They need to keep their innocence and have a childhood, and we can't have that when these pedophiles and their ideologies are running amuck and ruining this country."

The words don't make sense in my head, but the pain does. Even if she's spouting nonsense, whether she believes it's real or not, the reality of losing a child is very real and apparent.

I wish that protecting Robin didn't do that to her.

"You're hearing her, right? She's nuts." Scarlett's waiting for a reaction from me.

"I don't really want to watch this right now." I hand the phone back to her. It's definitely not what she wanted out of me.

She takes it back, but she doesn't keep quiet. "Why are you sad for her? She wasn't going to do the right thing, and even now she's spreading that dumb shit all around for the world to see. Both you and I know that what she's doing is hurting people like your son. Why can't you realize that?"

"I realize it." I really do, that's why we've been making this whole journey in the first place. That's not the problem. The problem's that... that's my wife. That's the woman I love. "I know her, and I know that she's really hurt that her child's disappeared. She loves Robin."

"I doubt it."

"Life's very complicated. You'll understand a bit more when you've got your own loved ones to look after."

Scarlett's a little taken aback by that. "Oh, because I'm a teenager I don't understand what you're going through?"

"Well, I think—"

"No, you listen to me here. I may not be an adult or married or whatever, but I'm a lot smarter than people give me credit for. I can tell that you're doubting who your wife is, but for some reason still cling onto the idea of who you think she is. She's shown her true colors and you've shown yours. All you need to do is finally take off those glasses that you were told you needed all your life—you don't need them. They just stopped you from seeing the picture clearly."

What she says takes me a minute to process, and it takes another minute for it to really sink into my skin.

"What are you questioning about her?"

More than I really want to be thinking about. "I... I remember her being so loving and understanding to everyone. She seemed like she looked past everyone's everything. If they were in need, she was going to help them. Even me."

"But you're realizing that's not the case. There's a prerequisite you never saw before."

"Don't make fun of me. I really didn't see it." I really thought she cared.

"You said she looked past everyone's everything, even you. What do you mean by that?"

I was hoping she hadn't caught on to that, but I knew she was going to. A part of me feels reluctant to say it, but something about Scarlett tells me she's different than a lot of people in my life. She's not going to judge my past like everyone else. I'm not sure why. "My parents weren't great people, and I spent most of my childhood in the foster system. Not the greatest upbringing to have, really. Carol was one of the first people to actually treat me like a human being."

"So... she took advantage of that. She love-bombed you, manipulated you, and then gaslit you about the manipulation until you were completely under her control, and through that made you into the version *she* wanted and wouldn't let you be who you are."

That's a lot of words, and none of them are sticking. "What?"

"Did you have any friends to talk to? Or did Carol shoo them all away?"

"Well... I never really had friends."

"Come on, you had friends at some point," Scarlett assumes. "Everyone does."

I want to say that's not the case, mostly because that's how I feel. "For a few years, I had two friends. They were fun and I loved them, but they weren't the greatest people."

"What do you mean, 'they weren't the greatest people'?"

"Well, Carol told me they were bad people. She was just looking out for me."

"What bad things did they do?"

"They encouraged bad behavior in me. Carol pointed it out to me and said I should stay away because they made me a bad person and were confusing me left and right."

"What were the bad behaviors? Just doing dumb pranks?"

"No, they were..." They were listening to my favorite band and hanging out with gay people. And when Carol and I were just friends, before we had started dating, it was my history of sleeping with and kissing boys.

Those aren't bad things. They're just "wrong" in Carol's eyes, and the Church's eyes, and now the government's eyes.

I was so happy back then.

Why did I throw that all away? Why did I let myself think that I was a terrible person just for liking when a boy kissed me?

"Did you ever have a choice in things? Or did you have to agree with whatever she said at the risk of her calling you a terrible husband, or whatever crazy things she'd spout?"

It's something along those lines. She would say she wanted to get pizza, and I would say I wasn't feeling it, and then she would complain how I never do things for her. Or I would want to play my favorite music in the car, but she would say it makes her feel uncomfortable or gives her a headache and tell me to change it, and if I said I wanted to keep listening to it, she would huff and say that I don't love her, and I would change the music because I never want her to think that I don't love her. I know what it's like to not be loved, and it's the worst feeling.

And then there was Robin, and she wouldn't even listen to what his needs were. His basic needs.

"I think," Scarlett begins, "that if she was ever in love with you, she wasn't in love with *you*—she was in love with the idea of you. More like the idea that she could form you into whatever she wanted. And yeah, that's probably hard to swallow, but like, it's better to hear it now and figure it out then go further in life and not ever know."

I never thought a sixteen-year-old would have more insight into my own life than me. As much as I want to deny the idea that my wife just wanted to control me, I couldn't deny the fact that everything started clicking together. It's like I was given the missing pieces of a puzzle that I thought I had completed. Now that I've fully put it together, it doesn't look like this heavenly picture I thought it was. It honestly looks like hell.

"How many choices have you actually gotten to make for yourself? Or for your family?"

I have to really think about that. I want to say when we got married, but I remember Carol pushing me to propose, and her sisters and parents did too. They even gave me the ring to propose to her with because they knew I wouldn't have been able to afford one at the time. That was after dating her for three months. Then I want to say that it was where we were going to move, and I said the city so that I could be close to work and we would have everything close, but Carol insisted that we move to a more rural area. I only eventually agreed because of the beautiful nature.

"Have you made any choices?" Scarlett starts looking concerned for me. At this point, I can't really blame her. I'm scaring myself a bit.

It takes a while to find one that I did make. "Running away with Robin is one."

"That's really the one choice that comes to your mind?"

I nod.

"Does your own son even know who you are? Do you even know who you are?"

"I know who I am. Robin knows who I am."

"What's your favorite band?"

"Green Day."

Scarlett's eyes go wide. "*You... like Green Day?*"

"Oh, I love Green Day."

"You've, like, actually listened to their music, right? Like the lyrics?"

"Oh, I used to scream them." Some of my favorite memories from those few friends I had were us just rocking out to that glorious music.

"Okay, we're gonna skip over that for a minute. Does he know you like Green Day?"

"Yeah."

"Has he heard any Green Day music?"

"Well..." I can feel the trap I'm falling into. "No. Carol would never allow that kind of music in the house."

"What's your favorite movie?"

"Probably *The Dark Knight.*"

"And has he seen it?"

I start feeling guilty about everything in my life. "No."

"Now, tell me, if a person says they like something, but you never really see them interact with it, do you really think that they like it? Or does it seem that they just say it?"

"I guess it wouldn't feel genuine."

"In my opinion, it makes you look like a hollow human. You'll talk like one and act like one, but you don't have passions or things you love. I can't imagine going about your whole life and not having things you love, or having things you love that you don't ever do or listen to or watch. That sounds so sad, and I don't understand why someone would deprive themselves of that joy willingly."

I guess when you think of it that way, it's so sad. And that is what I've done to myself, whether or not I really want to think about it. But... "There is one thing Robin knows I like."

"What's that?"

"The stars and nature. I've taught him all I know. I used to go outside and look at the stars when I was little. I was a little crazy back then. I was hungry for any fact I could get about the night sky." I can't help but chuckle a bit. I remember being little and going to the library and begging librarians for any books or anything they knew about stars. And I remember looking at the stars with different foster siblings and enjoying being around them and looking up there. Then there were nights when I'd be forced to sleep outside, and I was actually happy about it because then I got to spend the whole night stargazing.

I notice Scarlett smiling a bit, and that's when I realize I'm smiling just from reminiscing.

"So," Scarlett speaks up. "Green Day?"

I chuckle a bit. "It's been a while since I've listened to any of their stuff, but yeah. I loved them. Especially in my first year or so of college."

"That's crazy to me. Coming from a brainwashed Texas man."

"I mean... I don't like the term *brainwashed*."

"But let's be real, that's what you are. At least what you became with that woman around you."

I... well... it's true. "Just don't knock me for it. It's not as easy to avoid as you might think."

She wants to argue, but she closes her mouth. I'm glad she's able to.

"My childhood made me very anti-government," I tell her. "They just about failed me every way. Listening to their music kind of felt freeing, like I wasn't the only one that felt that way or the only one that realized it. That I wasn't wrong, I guess. Probably helped that I got shoved out of the foster system around the time I started really listening to them." Just talking about it takes a weight off my chest. I haven't felt like this since eighteen.

I haven't realized how much I miss being eighteen.

"Foster system's really f-ed up." Scarlett scowls. "Haven't had to deal with it, but I've heard stories. That's the government for you, I guess. They'll care about dumb shit but not the important things."

She has a very good point, and even though I don't know what my thoughts really are on anything now, I at least know what's kind of going on. I feel like I have to start from scratch and figure myself out all over again. I never noticed how much of me was just a forced extension of Carol, and starting over sounds so daunting.

But maybe I can get a bit of myself back. It sucks that I never knew I lost myself, but I guess Scarlett's right in saying that it's better to learn now than die and have still been just Carol's puppet.

Kids... Kids are pretty smart in their own way.

I'm glad Scarlett got stuck with us. I hope she's glad in some way too.

Chapter 21

Robin

 wake up to the train stopping in North Dakota. Dad says it's time for us to get off and get going, and that we have a lot of walking ahead of us.

We start almost immediately, coming out of Minot and into the bare wilderness that is North Dakota. We stay somewhat close to a road, but that road eventually becomes the only thing we see.

"Hey, Robin," Dad begins. He has a bit of a smile on his face. It's a lot bigger than I thought it could ever be. It sort of scares me a bit, even though I know he's just happy. "Do you remember what my favorite band is?"

"Green Day?"

"Yeah."

Though it's rare for him to bring it up, he always says his favorite band is Green Day.

"And I think you should hear some of their songs."

Where is he going with this? "How are we going to listen to music all the way out here?"

"Scarlett can play some music off her phone."

One of Scarlett's eyebrows rises. "You want me to risk my battery life to play some music?"

"Not just any music." Dad scoffs. "Green Day."

She doesn't seem moved by that.

"Come on. Please? Only 'till the battery gets low, then we'll put it away."

Even though I think it's a little silly that we're going to use our only phone for music, I'm also curious what kind of music Dad likes. I don't really know much about the music he talks about. Talk about it all you want, it doesn't give a good idea of what it sounds like.

Scarlett decides to give in. "Fine. Gimme a second."

It takes her a minute, and even though her phone isn't the loudest thing in the world, the music begins to play. Right at the get go, I'm blown by the loud and fast guitars and the pounding beat of the drums. I actually really like the melody too as it makes my body fill up with energy. Energy I need to get out some way, like running around or dancing to it or something. I just need to do something!

Dad must've been feeling the same because he picks me up and starts spinning around, making both him and I a little dizzy as he screams the lyrics at the top of his lungs. I hear Scarlett laugh, but all I can see is Dad's energy and smile. It's the most I've seen in him in a week. No, not a week. I think it's the happiest I've ever seen him.

When spinning becomes terrible for both of us, we kinda just jump and headbang to the song. All the while, he's still singing every single lyric. It's like he knows it by heart. It's so awesome to see Dad like this. I wish he was like this a lot more. It's so fun to just goof off and be silly. Even Scarlett joins in on just letting it all out. We're all just going through the wilderness goofing off and having so much fun with our little camaraderie of three.

Kinda like Robin Hood and his gang of Merry Men.

Not only does that make me the happiest, but seeing Dad be silly and happy makes it even better. It's contagious, and I never realized what people meant when they said that till now.

At some point, Dad says some lyrics that makes Scarlett absolutely lose it. A chuckle bursts from her mouth before she's able to get anything words out. "Oh my god! You can't say that word! You're not gay."

"Can I use it if I made out with a boy in high school?"

Scarlett's jaw drops. So does mine, in all honesty. "You're telling me you made out with another guy before?"

"Yeah," Dad says nonchalantly. He really doesn't care about anything. It makes me giggle a bit. I don't know what happened to Dad overnight, but I love it.

"Well, did you like it? Because if you liked it, you're gay." A little smirk starts spreading on Scarlett's face.

"Oh, I loved it."

Scarlett hunches over, cackling at what Dad said. Honestly I can't believe it either. This is absolutely insane! Am I dreaming? There's no way Dad's like this. This is too crazy to be happening.

"Robin, sing with me!" He grabs me by the arms and starts swinging me around.

"But I don't know the lyrics."

"It's fine, they kind of repeat themselves."

And when the chorus comes, we both scream it at the top of our lungs about how messed up everything became because of how they say things on the news. How they make it so everyone should be scared and just do as they're told. And how we aren't going to become an "American Idiot."

Who knew how fun it is to scream about rebelling against society and its dumb rules!

Eventually the phone has to be put away, but that doesn't stop us from having fun. I ask if we can play Robin Hood, and after explaining it to Scarlett, she agrees. So we pretend to gallop through the forests of Sherwood. For some reason, Dad decides his horse is the fastest, even though there's no race. It's hard to get him to slow down, but eventually he gets his horse to listen. Scarlett's horse is the most obedient. It's also the most graceful. She says she just trained it to be that way, but there's no way that's possible. If it was, I would've trained mine to be like that.

We walk for hours and hours and hours. It's so long that eventually the sun sets and the moon starts to show. My feet are aching from walking all day and I'm so tired that I feel like I'm gonna fall asleep any moment. Dad says that he can carry me for a while and I can rest. He promises that he'll wake me up when we cross the border so I can enjoy the moment. As he picks me up and puts his green jacket on me like it's a blanket, I feel my eyelids droop. Before I know it, I fall asleep with my head on Dad's shoulder.

***

"Robin! Robin, wake up." Dad's voice echoes in my head. I assume we're about to cross the border, so I try my best to wake up. It's hard to even open my eyes, though.

"Are we there?"

"Sort of. We've still got a ways to go, but you need to get on your feet."

"Why?" I ask. There's the sound of a car driving in the distance. Are we still by the road?

"They're getting closer!" I hear Scarlett's voice.

I'm finally able to open my eyes a bit, and when I do, I see a car in the distance. Its lights are really bright.

"I don't think they can see us quite yet, but we need to get going. Robin, I'm gonna put you down now, okay?"

"Okay." I suddenly feel very awake.

Dad puts me down, and once my feet are on the ground, he grabs my hand and starts running.

Not a minute later, police sirens start piercing the dead of the night. I can see the red and blue lights shine from behind, its claws reaching out for us. It lights up some of the path ahead, and I can see lots of trees.

Dad looks behind us. He doesn't slow down one bit as our feet slam against the ground. My feet ache with every step, begging me to stop, but my heart's telling me to keep running and not think of anything else other than running.

"How much further?" I ask Dad. I'm trying my best to not freak out, but I can feel some tears come into my eyes as dread starts seeping into my veins.

"Just keep running," is all he says. "Hold Scarlett's hand. I'll be behind to make sure nothing happens, okay?"

I don't like the idea, but Dad makes Scarlett take my hand, and I notice that he slows down a bit. I can hear a thousand different alarms screaming in my head on top of the loud sirens that are disturbing the night. I look behind to make sure Dad's still with us, and he is. He once again tells me, "just keep running."

But I notice the car is getting bigger and bigger, and the sirens are getting louder and louder. It's like someone's trying to get into my head and they're doing so by stabbing a knife into my skull, hoping to cut through the bone.

Scarlett doesn't say anything; she's just going. And she's going a lot faster than Dad. I don't know if that's how she runs or if the moment just gives her the superpower to run so fast. It's hard to keep up with her. I swear we're going so fast that I'm nervous I'll trip or my legs are gonna fall off. I'm so scared that I'll fall or slip and screw us all up. I can't mess up; if I mess up, we're all in trouble, and the thought that I might cause that is something I don't want to happen.

I hear someone say something, but I can't catch what it is. Their voice is loud, and it's someone I don't recognize. I look back for a second to see someone from the car sticking their head out and using a megaphone.

"Robin, don't look back, just keep running! We're almost there. Once we're there, they can't chase us," Dad assures me. I don't think twice and look forward, trying to focus on the ground ahead of me, making sure I don't trip on an anthill or the root of a tree.

I gotta run. I gotta run. I gotta run.

Just keep running.

I hear a loud bang, and I know exactly what that sound is. I grew up hearing it, and I don't need to look back to see that it is a gun.

I try really hard to do what Dad told me, I really do. Scarlett's not afraid of the sound. She just keeps running as if it had never happened. I'm still running with her, but I have to look back to see what is going on.

Before I can look at anything, Dad yells at me, "Robin, r—"

Then a gunshot echoes throughout the entire world.

And Dad falls to the ground, mid-stride.

And his body just lays there.

"Dad!" I scream as my world grows blurry. I swear I see him twitch a bit, or attempt to get up as I try running to him, but Scarlett grabs my hand and picks me up as quick as she can. I try to get a view of my father, but I can't tell what's going on as Scarlett runs to the border while the entire world shakes and screams and blinds me.

Chapter 22

Robin

e just barely make it to Canada before they can get to us. And even then, Scarlett keeps running until the cars are far in the distance. She doesn't slow down for a long time.

She's out of breath and about to collapse when she finally stops and puts me down. Once I'm on the ground, she lays down and takes a moment to breathe.

I just sit there and cry.

A part of me can't believe what I just saw. What just happened? He was fine one second and the next he was on the ground. He must've tripped. I look over to where America is, hoping I can see Dad in the distance. He has to be. I didn't see him fully get up, but I know he wouldn't leave us. He's going to be here soon.

"Robin, what are we going to do?" Scarlett's voice somehow reaches my ear. I can't get myself to say anything as she gets up and comes over to me. "Hey, what are we going to do? We're in Canada, now what do we do?"

"We have to wait for Dad!"

"We can't do that."

"We can't leave him behind. He'll be here soon. I need Dad."

"Robin, your dad's not coming. He got grabbed by the cops."

I don't remember seeing it, but the more I think about how little Dad was moving, the more I realize that the cops did probably grab him. They must've done something to stop him and make him fall. What's going to happen to him? I can't imagine that it would be anything good because they were chasing and shooting at us. I hope they don't hurt him. I hope he's gonna be okay. "Do you think Dad will be okay?"

"I don't know."

"We gotta help him! How can we help him?" Dad helped me when I was hurt—I gotta return the favor. I can't do this without Dad! I can't do this on my own! I need him! And right now, he needs me!

"Robin, there's nothing we can do! Right now, we've got to figure out what we're doing next."

But I can't ignore Dad! I... I guess it's true there's nothing we can do, but I just can't forget that he's hurt and in trouble. Why couldn't he get pass the border with us? Why did he have to get taken?

"Now, what's the next step? What was your dad gonna do once we got here?"

It takes me a minute to clear my head enough to answer her question. "I don't know."

"Come on. Didn't your dad tell you what he was going to do?"

"He didn't tell me anything! He wouldn't let me know." The tears start coming faster, and I can feel them go down my cheek two at a time.

"He had to have said something!"

"He said he was going to get a job, but he didn't say anything else!"

Scarlett groans at hearing that. "Well, why—" She stops herself before she can say anything more. The world's still pretty blurry but I can see her pace. I feel really bad that I don't know how to help. I don't know how to help Dad and I don't know how to help Scarlett. I know it's not my fault, but if I knew what Dad's plan was, we wouldn't be worrying about what to do. And Scarlett wouldn't be mad about everything. It takes her a minute to calm down and figure out what we're going to do. "Okay. We're going to find a town, and then we'll figure it out from there. Except... I don't know where any of the towns are and my phone's dead thanks to your dad wanting to listen to music."

It's quiet between the two of us. I don't know what to do or say.

"To be clear, there's no town your dad talked about?"

I shake my head.

"Well, how do we find a town?"

I don't know. I look up to the sky and can make out Polaris all the way in the north. It somehow hurts to look at the star and makes me want to cry more. It reminds me too much of Dad and his love of the stars. And how much he did for me and all the things he's taught me. Like how to be a man.

Maybe... maybe I know how to get us somewhere.

"We can go north. We just follow Polaris."

"What good is that gonna do? We've been going north for forever."

"We're bound to hit something eventually," I try to say between my sobs. "A town, a road, something. Dad said if you don't know where you are, follow water, which we can't go to because that's too close to America. Then follow power lines, which there aren't really any around either. If there's no water or power lines, then just go north. And Polaris is always north." I point to where the star is in the sky so Scarlett can see where it is.

She doesn't seem very convinced by the idea, but I think she does agree that it's better than nothing. "Okay then. Do you think you can walk or are you too tired?"

I am tired, and I don't want to do anything but be with Dad, but I know that right now I'm not going to get that. "I can."

"Alright, let's get going then."

With that, we start walking. It's pretty cold, the air biting at my skin, but I at least have Dad's jacket. I'm so thankful to have it because it makes me feel a little warmer. I feel bad about it a bit because Scarlett looks so cold, but she assures me that she's fine. She just puts her arm around me and says that our combined heat is enough.

The two of us walk for hours. We don't really talk much. I can only really cry and Scarlett has the smarts to realize that there's no point in starting a conversation. She just comforts me with her constant side hug and presence, which is enough to keep me going for the time being.

Eventually we find a road, and then follow it to a small town. The town is so small, only a few houses are there. It's a little sad to see, but I guess it's something rather than nothing.

Scarlett tells me to sit by one of the houses as she pulls out whatever food we have left from my bag. It's not a lot, but it's a good amount. It doesn't help with how tired we are, though.

I swear one second it's dark outside, and then the next second the sun has risen and there's a man threatening to call the cops. I get really scared and start crying again. Scarlett tries to explain to the guy, but it doesn't stop him.

Before the cops get to town, Scarlett makes two things very clear. One is that she's going to stand behind me, and that I should not be afraid of that. It's so we both are going to be safe. The other is that when the police come to make it extremely clear that we are asylum-seekers. She says that the best thing we can do is be completely honest. I don't like the idea of that. Being honest seems like the way to get sent all the way back home.

The police came, and thankfully the sirens aren't going off. As they get out of the car, Scarlett immediately puts her hands up in the air and yells, "we're seeking asylum!"

I know that's my cue. "We're asylum-seekers!" I put my hands in the air too because I think that's what I'm supposed to do. I can feel the tears running down my cheeks again. And I see a gun at the police-woman's side, and it gets hard to breathe. I feel like my lungs are getting tighter, and my head starts feeling light, kinda like when I was sick all the way back home.

"Robin." Scarlett nudges me. "Answer her question."

I didn't even know that she said something to me. "What is it?"

"Where are you seeking asylum from?"

"The- The U.S." I feel so terrible sobbing on my own words in front of her. I hope it doesn't get us hurt.

"Are you his guardian?" the woman asks Scarlett.

"No, I'm just a friend who was with them."

"Them?"

"His dad was with us, but he isn't now."

"I see. What is your name?" she asks me first.

"Robin Wright," is the first thing that I say, then I realize I have to be honest about everything. I hate that I have to say this. "Well, legally, it's Grace Wright, but I go by Robin."

The policewoman gives me a look, and I'm afraid that it's the end of it all for us. She looks at Scarlett. "And you?"

"Scarlett Lane Brooks. I have a driver's license if you wanna see it."

The policewoman debates with herself for a moment. "Let me see."

Scarlett only puts her hand down so she can grab her wallet. She shows the license, which looks like her in the photo and says her name and everything. It's legit.

"Do you have a passport?"

"No I do not."

"Well then, take off your bags and face the wall. The both of you are under arrest and coming with me."

Under arrest? No, I can't go to jail. I'm just trying to live! Does wanting to live really end up putting me in jail?

"Where are you taking us?" Scarlett demands, but does as she's told. I do the same as her.

The policewoman never answers the question.

I hate the feeling of the cold metal handcuffs around my wrists. It also feels so uncomfortable to have my hands behind my back, and I'm getting scared that I'm going to need to move my arms but won't be able to.

Scarlett gets taken into the car first, and then me. Our bags are put somewhere else, which concerns me because I don't want to lose any of my stuff.

Scarlett and I are thrown into the backseat, which has bars all around it. The idea of being in a place where I'm trapped and surrounded by bars starts getting into my head. It's reminding me of TV shows that the bad guys always get put in after they finally get caught by the good guys. But I'm not a bad guy; I'm a good guy. Scarlett's a good guy. Dad's a good guy. Why did Dad get hurt and taken? That only happens to bad guys! Why are Scarlett and I going to jail? That only happens to bad guys!

Scarlett leans over to me. "It's okay. You're going to be fine." I know that if she could move her arms, she would give me a hug. Since she can't, she just sits close to me and lets me cry onto her jacket as I have the longest car ride of my life.

When we eventually stop, the officer opens the door and drags both me and Scarlett out of the car and into a building. My eyes are still too blurry to read any signs that say what it is.

We're made to sit in a room. I'm not really paying attention to anything. I can't get myself to pay attention to anything. All I can do is really cry.

But then I hear Dad's name.

As fast as I can, I do all I can to stop crying, rubbing my knees against my eyes so that I can wipe the tears away while my hands are still cuffed behind my back. Once my sight is clear enough, I look around to see who's talking about Dad. How do they know Dad?

I first look at the officer, but she's talking about something else with someone. There's a few other people, but I can't hear them well enough from where I sit, so I don't think they said his name.

The only other thing was the TV. I look up at it, finding the news playing, and it's some video taken from a helicopter, I think. Most of it's dark and you can't see much aside from a few police cars and some lights shining down on a few people that are running.

And then I see the news headline.

Child groomer and predator announced dead

No...

"Mr. Wright was wanted for multiple counts, including emotional and sexual abuse of his eleven-year-old daughter, Grace, on top of the charge of kidnapping her. Last night, a police department in North Dakota, U.S.A, finally located and pursued him after days of no leads and were finally able to catch him. It seems that Wright was attempting to run to Canada, where he would've been able to run away from the charges. Thankfully, Officer Gisbourne had the sense to shoot on sight, not only preventing Wright from getting out of jurisdiction, but also from preventing him from hurting any more children. Richard Wright was pronounced dead at the scene."

No!

As the clip plays, you can see one of the people that's running fall, but all I can see is Dad just dropping right in front of me. Somehow all the chairs and walls and people disappear and I'm just standing there in a dark cold field, seeing Dad behind me, hearing his voice telling me to keep running. Just keep running! And then I hear a shot so loud, I swear the whole world shakes with it.

And Dad falls to the ground, mid-stride.

And his body just lays there.

Now all I can see is how still he is. He's not moving. He's not breathing. He's just a corpse. He dies just like that. As if someone snaps their fingers and makes him stop breathing just like that. It's so quick. One second he's there, and another it's like he's been replaced with a dead body. How can that happen? How can someone die so quickly? And there was no trying to figure things out—it just ended him in a matter of a second!

But now I can't really tell if that was what happened, or if I'm mixing some parts of the story up, or if I'm making up others. It's like living in a sandcastle. It was a thing that existed so clearly, then the waves came, and all I have left is the crowning shell that was put on the top of that castle made of sand.

The only problem about that shell is that it's Dad dying right in front of me.

Dad... Dad's gone.

"And as you can see from the video provided by the police force, not only was he running away, but it seems that he had two children with him, likely more victims of his grooming. Neither of which are his daughter. The police have confirmed that Grace Wright has still not been found, and considering that Richard Wright is dead and the two children in his possession have not been caught, it is possible that we may never find or know what happened to little Grace Wright."

Dad's dead. They killed him! All because he was protecting me and keeping me safe. All because he did the right thing.

Even though I'm still in the darkness of the field, I feel like someone's wrapping me up in a hug. I think it's Scarlett, and even though I feel the hug and hear her voice mutter in the wind, all I can see for miles and miles is myself, the dark plain field, and Dad's lifeless corpse.

Chapter 23

Robin

fter Scarlett calms me down, we go somewhere that the officers around us insist is not a jail or a prison; it's simply a "detention center." I'm pretty sure they're lying, but I can't tell if it's really for my comfort or theirs.

When we get there, I'm asked a lot of questions, and a lot of invasive ones. It's mostly about my gender, and I don't know how to explain it because I try telling them I'm transgender, but they keep rewording and rephrasing so I'm forced to say I was born a girl. And once I say that, they just keep calling me a girl. It doesn't matter how many times I try to explain to them that I'm a boy, or how many times Scarlett corrects them, they just keep doing it!

Surely this can't be better than home.

The only good thing about it is that I get to stay with Scarlett. Not that I really would let them have a choice. Scarlett's the only person I know, and I know that she'll stand up for me. I don't care if I'm making a ruckus, I just need someone I know with me! Even if I don't know her all that well. I don't want to be alone in a completely different country. Or rather, a completely different world.

We spend a whole day in the prison. The only thing we really do is talk to this one person who says they're going to help represent us. I'm not sure what they mean. Other than that, there's nothing to do, and I start wondering how long we're going to be there. I hope not long. I don't want to be stuck here. Even though it's quiet and still, it feels like so much is happening, and so much of it feels so surreal. The world is quiet, but everything in my head feels so loud. I don't know how to think or feel about any of it.

The next day, we finally get to explain everything to someone. Technically Scarlett and I are supposed to go in separately, but the idea of Scarlett not being in my eyesight makes me so scared that I think I'm gonna cry and throw up. Not having her and being in a room with a stranger, or sitting by myself in the prison makes me want to burst, so they let us both go at the same time.

When we come in, there are a few different people, but one man stands out from the rest. When he sees the both of us, he smiles. "Hello. I'm Mr. Lea. A pleasure to meet you." He puts his hand out for us to shake.

"Scarlett." The two of them shake hands.

Then he holds out his hand for me to shake. Since Scarlett did it, I think it's fine. "Robin."

"Robin?" He quirks a brow. If he's anything like everyone else around here, he's going to call me a girl.

"It's not my legal name, I know, but it's what I like to go by, so please call me that."

"He's transgender," Scarlett explains.

Hearing that word brings Mr. Lea great joy, a peculiar smile spreading across his face. I don't know why, because most people hear that word and feel anything but happy about it. "Oh, that's perfect. And you guys came from America?"

"We did."

"And the both of you are trying to get refugee status?"

"Yes."

"Any relation to Robin here? Or any claims for why you should be eligible?"

"I'm just a friend, but I'm a lesbian. I got picked up while they were on their way. A family friend set up the whole thing in probably like five minutes."

"Alright. I see it now. Two queer kids running from America as she shows her true colors as the fascist country she's always been. With the new Families Come First Act, it's bound to get attention. Why, your case could in theory be a landmark for thousands of other kids like you."

I don't want to be in some big court case; I just want to get out of here. I just want to be safe and be a boy. I know it wasn't possible back home, but can I just have that simple thing here? Can I just have that and not have to go through some long hard process or journey to get that?

I just want to be a kid. Is that so much to ask?

"Now, take a seat and tell me the whole story from the top. There might be more I can use. The more you tell me and the more honest you are, the more I can assure you that I can get you out of this detention center so you can live your life in Canada."

Scarlett doesn't discourage me. She stays right by my side, and even has her arm out for me to hold.

I tell him everything, starting from last Christmas. The more agony and suffering that spills out of me, the more tears that come. At some point, it becomes too much, and I can't speak. Mr. Lea assures me that I can take a break.

While I'm crying and hugging Scarlett, our lawyer asks her about her part of the story. She explains how she was born and raised in Chicago, which although pretty liberal, was subjected to the same laws I was back in Texas because things were getting passed on a national scale. She's a lot more articulate with her answers. She uses words like *unconstitutional*, which makes her sound very smart. I'm so glad that I have her by my side.

Apparently, her family knows she's a lesbian, and pretty chill about it. I'm surprised to hear that. Considering she's running away, I thought she was in the same boat as me. Her parents, as well as the rest of her family, are aware that she left and that she's heading to Canada for her safety because of some law that was passed. I feel bad for her because she sounds really close with her family, and she had to leave them just because she's afraid she would be jailed and killed.

I feel a little guilty leaving Mom, and I feel absolutely devastated to have lost Dad. I can only wonder how she feels about having to say goodbye to her whole family because she doesn't want to die over her being a lesbian.

Soon enough, it's back on me unfortunately. I try to finish as best I can, but then I start blubbering again, so Scarlett ends up finishing the story.

As I cry, the lawyer smirks. "How fascinating! Seems the two of you have been on quite a journey. And, just double checking, your father was Richard Wright? The American that was all over the news the past week?"

Scarlett speaks up for me since I can't really get any words out. "Yes, that was him."

"So you're his child that he allegedly kidnapped, among other things?"

I hate that all those disgusting lies are being tied to my dad's name. He doesn't deserve that! "He was protecting me!" I scream at Mr. Lea, all my tears spilling out of me.

"Yes, yes, that's why I said, 'allegedly.' It's a fancy word for saying that there are people who have said things that may or may not be true about your father."

I don't care if it's alleged or not, my father should never be called those things! He was a good man and his name shouldn't be tainted.

"And, the best thing is that you get to tell the whole world that."

That makes me feel better, but I also have an odd feeling in my gut. Something's not right. Maybe... because that would mean that Mom would hear about it. "But what about Mom? If she hears, she's gonna try and take me back. I can't go back!"

"Don't worry. Your anonymity is one of my top priorities. I wouldn't be a good lawyer if I didn't focus on your protection, would I?"

I guess that is true.

"No one is going to know your real name during the trial and the journalists won't either. I promise."

I'm still scared. Something about all of it doesn't feel right. And the fact that I don't have Dad to be there and fight for me makes it even worse.

Chapter 24

Robin

he audio of the video crackles throughout the courtroom as it plays. I don't know if I'm going to be able to watch it. I don't really want to be here. Why did I agree to being here?

In the video, you can see me fidget with Dad's jacket as I'm trying to remember everything that Mr. Lea told me to say. The memories of doing take after take start pounding my head because I would mess one thing up and we'd have to do the whole thing over.

"My name is Robin Wright. I'm eleven years old and I'm from Texas, United States of America. I am transgender. Last Christmas, I started experiencing gender dysphoria, and because of that, I got really sick."

You can see the tears welling up in my eyes. I tried so hard to not cry in that moment, and I thought I was doing a great job at the time, but watching now, you can tell I was fighting it.

"When my parents found out, my mom sent me to a correctional facility, and it was the worst thing I could've ever been put through."

I honestly don't remember much about the facility. I was too sick to do anything, let alone remember it. I just remember no one caring that I was dying before their eyes. Mr. Lea told me to talk about the facility because it was technically the truth and that it would help my case.

"My dad, Richard Wright, pulled me out of there and helped me get better. Not only was it possible for my mother to put me in a place like that, but it was highly recommended, and has recently become a requirement across the country—putting kids like me in even more danger than we are already in. I was very lucky to have someone to save me, and it was my dad's idea to run to Canada because it was no longer safe for me back home."

A tear slips out of my eye and down my cheek, first in the video, then as I sit in the courtroom.

Oh, Dad, I miss you so much.

You did so much just for me.

"If I had stayed in America, I would have likely died in the correction facility that I was placed in, or I would've been arrested for just being transgender, and held in prison or maybe even quietly executed for simply being a kid who knew who he was."

The tears start flowing in the video, and I realize that it looks like I'm crying because I was scared at the idea of dying in those ways.

I mean, I am, but I don't think anyone could understand how much those tears were for Dad. He saved me from all of that. He did everything; he gave his life for the possibility of me being safe somewhere else.

My dad died so I didn't.

I start crying as much as I am in the video.

"And that is, even if I survived gender dysphoria and the lack of resources that transgender people have in America. The lack of having hormones or hormone blockers, or simply the inability to go by a different name and pronoun might have killed me first."

Dad, I love you so much. I wish you were still here. I don't want to be alone and do all of this alone. How am I gonna do anything? How am I gonna learn how to build a shelter, or start a fire? How am I gonna become strong? I feel anything but strong right now. How am I gonna learn to be a man when I don't have you to teach me?

I'm never gonna play catch with you. I'm never gonna go camping with you. I'm never gonna watch sports with you. I'm never gonna do fun projects with you. I'm never gonna have you to talk to. I'm never gonna have you make a joke that will annoy me. I'm never gonna have you do something dumb and make me smile when I'm sad. I'm never gonna have you show me how to stand for what's right and what I believe in.

I'm never gonna have you.

Never ever again.

I think I miss the end of the video because I'm crying. The next thing I remember is being put on a stand and answering questions.

"Now, according to American media, your father was wanted for crimes involving predatory behaviors," someone says to me during questioning. I don't remember who it is. I just remember wanting to scream at them that they are wrong. It's really hard to be civil in the courtroom, but Mr. Lea told me that if I'm civil in this, I wouldn't have to be so much longer. "Had your father ever touched you in an inappropriate way?"

"No." I make sure my no is very firm because it's disgusting that they would even think that.

"Had your father ever made comments about your body?"

"No. I hadn't ever heard of him talking about things like that." It's the truth. I think I know what the man is alluding to, but I'm not entirely sure. Whatever it is, I know that my dad wouldn't dare think of doing things like that to me. I know that for a fact. He wouldn't have wanted to hurt me, past or present, if he had risked so much.

"Well, then, how can the American charges be explained?"

"Objection, foundational issues, your honor," Mr. Lea begins. "Simply put, those American charges aren't fully true, least not to our standards. Yes, Richard Wright had charges against him, including grooming and child abuse, but in recent years, the definition of that in America includes parents who are trying to get their transgender children proper healthcare in the form of hormone replacement therapy. And, as Robin Wright had beautifully described in his original testimony, hormone replacement therapy is an absolutely life-saving treatment for transgender children that has unfortunately been outlawed in the United States. While yes, Richard Wright's charges are concerning, we do need to look at it and perceive it through an American lens."

"Well, if possible, I would still like to ask, Robin—had your father ever hurt you in any way?"

"No. He would never do that." Neither of my parents hit me, but especially not Dad. Mom had hurt me, though she would probably deny that. Dad never meant to hurt me, and the only way he had hurt me was through his silence over the course of the years, and that was because at that point he was getting hurt too.

I don't think I ever realized he was getting hurt. I kinda wonder how bad it was, but only because I think he had to go through a lot to be shut up.

"Let's move away from Robin's father," the judge declares.

"Well, then, Robin," the person I can't remember starts. "What of your mother? Why can't you go live with her?"

"She was the one who sent me to the correction facility. And she had hurt me and said terrible things to me."

"What things?"

I all of a sudden can't remember. I just remember how I felt when she said those things, but not what she actually said. "She would make me wear dresses and I would feel like I had spiders crawling all over my body, and she would say I was confused and act like I was being immature or like I was five-years-old. She would insist that I was a girl when I had told her I was a boy and everything she would say would just make me sicker and sicker! And she never brought me to a hospital when I was throwing up constantly—she just brought me to the doctor once, was told I had the flu, and then did nothing else about it. Then she sent me to a camp that wasn't going to do anything for me but make me worse!"

I start crying on the stand, and I feel so embarrassed and naked. Here I am in this room with all these adults and strangers that I don't know and I have to spill out the worst parts of my life in front of them so that they can decide if I can live in a country that's safe or to send me back to my home where I will be killed.

I'm just a kid, and I have to talk about the time that I was so sick that it was traumatic, and talk about how my Dad—who put everything on the line—died, and try to explain to them that he wasn't some fricking pervert and talk about how I've almost died and all the different ways that I can die all for them to possibly send me back to hell and be brutally murdered?

What the... What the fuck is this world?

Fuck the world!

Fuck it all!

Chapter 25

Robin

 don't remember much more about the trial. I just remember that Scarlett was so happy for me and gave me the biggest hug at the end of it. We are both allowed to stay, but that doesn't really make me feel different about everything.

Scarlett and I go back to the jail, but only to grab our stuff that had been taken a few days ago when we got arrested. It's so nice to get it all back, especially because my copy of *The Merry Adventures* is in there. I don't know what I would do if it wasn't there. It's the book that Dad got me before we left... almost a week ago.

It hasn't even been a week since I've left home.

As we wait for some people to come, I sit close to Scarlett and try to read *The Merry Adventures* in the front office. I can't really get myself to focus on it, though. Somehow, I can't form the grass and trees of Sherwood Forest or see Robin Hood very clearly. Even though I really just want to transport myself away from where I am, I can't seem to disappear from the real world.

We watch a few different people come in and out over the next hour or so. Scarlett's more focused on watching people and seeing if they are here for us than I am. At some point, it pays off because after talking with the lady at the front desk, a woman comes over. She smiles. "Which one of you is Robin?"

I'm a little hesitant to say something, and only do so once Scarlett gives me a nod. "I am."

"Nice to meet you. My name is Ms. Elizabeth, and I'm here to take you to a place where you're gonna live for a while."

"Is it a good place?"

"It's a very good place. And it's only temporary. Now, do you have all your things?"

I nod.

"Great. Let's get going then." She holds out her hand for me to grab. Even though I don't want to, I do as she wishes. I get up, and we start walking to the door.

Right before we're about to leave, I realize something. I turn around to find that Scarlett is still sitting by the desk, waiting.

"Ms. Elizabeth!" I pat her arm to get her attention. "What about Scarlett?"

"Hmm?"

"What about Scarlett?" I point over to my friend.

"Oh, she's not coming with us."

She's not?

No! I need her! I don't want to leave her!

I let go of Ms. Elizabeth and run back over to Scarlett. I give her the fiercest hug I can and hold tightly onto her. If I hold on tight enough then they can't rip me away from her.

Scarlett sighs. "Robin—"

"No, I'm not leaving you." I want to make my stance clear. "Why aren't you coming with me?"

"I'm old enough to be on my own. It would just work out better for me."

"But then I'll never see you again." I'm not ready to lose her. She's the only one that knows what I've gone through, and she's the only one that's been so nice and looked out for me. I wouldn't have gotten this far without her, and I feel so safe around her, and I don't want to be alone. I don't want to be alone in a whole new world, a world where I don't know anything that's going on.

"Well... maybe I can visit." She's able to pry me off enough where she can look me in the eye. Even though I'm crying, she's pretty calm. "I can find out where you're going, and then I'll come and visit."

"Can you visit every day? Please?"

"I'll have to see what my new schedule would be, but I'll try to visit when I can."

"Promise?"

"Promise."

Her saying that makes me feel a little bit better. Not a lot, but a little bit. I'm still gonna be stuck in a different world, alone.

Ms. Elizabeth is kind enough to tell Scarlett where I'm going, but after that, there's no way to stall anymore. So for what I'm scared is the final time, Scarlett says, "goodbye."

"Goodbye," I tell her as a tear slips out of my eye. And then Ms. Elizabeth makes me get in a car, and we drive somewhere that feels so far away from my friend.

***

It's been a few weeks since I moved into the orphanage, and it hasn't been the greatest.

The first day was fine because I was new and all the other kids were introducing themselves and being really nice. But after the first night, no one wanted to talk to me because I had some sort of nightmare that made me scream in my sleep. No one really wants to be friends with the kid who wakes the whole orphanage up. And the staff started getting more and more mean towards me because I would keep having nightmares almost every night.

But I guess it's all better than dying in America.

The only good thing about all of this is that Scarlett kept her promise. She comes to visit almost every day. Some days she can't because of work and other things, but I'm grateful she's even able to visit. I do wish that she could be with me the whole time, but I'm glad I even get to see her.

And today, thankfully, is no different.

"Hey, Robin, look what I brought today." Scarlett comes into my room, a big smile on her face. I wonder what it could possibly be considering how happy she is.

She pulls out something from her backpack, then hands it to me. It's a stuffed animal, a horse specifically.

"Whatcha think? Now you got your own trusty horse, just like Robin Hood."

I know it's her trying to be nice, so I smile. It doesn't really make me feel all that happy. I don't know if anything really would. "Thank you. How did you get this?"

"I got my first paycheck, so I decided to get something for you."

"Don't you need to pay for your new apartment?"

"Yeah, but right now I got some money to assist me with that. And I know that it sucks to be here by yourself, so I want to help you feel better."

I know anything I say won't sway her, so I nod.

"Wanna see some new photos that I took yesterday?"

She had told me that she was hanging out with a friend to take photos around town. I didn't know the friend, but he seems nice and I do want to see more of Scarlett's photos. "Yeah."

With a grin, she pulls out her phone and searches through it for a second before finding where she wants to start. "Here. This is him, and you can look at any photos onward from there."

He looks like a nice guy, and as Scarlett shows me the other photos, it's like getting a view of the most magical city in the world. I never thought that a city could be magical too. I always thought they were boring and dull because you can't see the stars, but the buildings look cool, like the old brick ones. I know that it's only the old buildings that look like that, but some parts of the city are old, and it's cool that some of it's still around.

"And this is the LGBTQ center I was talking about." She shows me a photo of a building that's so colorful and pretty, and it has the flag of progress in it's window. It's probably the most magical building in the whole world.

"Do you think you can take me there sometime? Or maybe you could just take me to the city? Just for a day."

"I don't know. I'd have to figure out if they would let me take you out of here."

Hearing that gives me my answer. They will never let me out of here on account of my nightmares, especially not with Scarlett, because she's only sixteen.

"Hey, how about I show you some more photos? There's a few from a park I went to that you would love."

She's not wrong about that. I love her nature photos.

Before she can get to them, there's a knock on the door, and I notice that one of the caretakers is here. "Robin, you have some visitors waiting for you."

I'm confused. "But Scarlett's already here."

"There are other visitors today. You don't know them, but they want to meet you."

Who would want to meet me?

"Can I send them in?"

I'm a little nervous, but also curious. "Sure."

"Alrighty then. Scarlett, how about you come with me."

Before she can even get up and leave, I hold on tightly to her. "No! Scarlett needs to stay." I don't think I can meet whoever these strangers are without her in the room. And I want her to stay in case something happens.

The caretaker looks like she's going to argue with me for a minute, but decides not to, a little begrudgingly. "Fine. I'll send the visitors in."

She leaves the room, and I get a little ball of anxiety in my stomach. I can feel it tangle itself, and I get scared about who's going to come through the door. It's someone I don't know, so I doubt it's someone who's going to try and take me back to America, but at the same time, I don't know who it is.

A man and a woman walk through the door. When they see me, they smile. The woman, who looks really beautiful, is the first to speak. "Hi, Robin."

I don't really know what to say, but I guess the first thing to start with is, "hi."

"I'm Mrs. Friar. And this is my husband, Mr. Friar."

"Hi," I say to Mr. Friar. He doesn't say anything, but he gives me a small, friendly wave.

"Who's this with you?" Mrs. Friar asks.

"This is Scarlett. She's a friend of mine."

"Nice to meet you, Scarlett. Are you also from—"

"No," she speaks up. "I'm just visiting Robin. I have my own place and I'm getting my footing."

"I see. You two seem pretty close."

Scarlett's quiet for a moment. "I guess we are."

"So, Robin, what do you like to do?"

I'm a little surprised by the question. I'm not really sure. "I... I like to read. And I want to learn how to do archery. Archery seems pretty cool."

"Have you ever done it before?"

"I don't think so." It's kinda hard to remember everything before I came here. It's so weird. It's like everything back in Texas was a different life that I might have lived, but I can't tell if I did.

"Are there any other things you like?"

"I really like nature. I love the stars and looking at them." They remind me of Dad, and even though it makes me cry every time, it feels so nice to see them.

"Oh, that's perfect. We live on a horse ranch a little ways away from town. The stars are beautiful from there. And it looks like you love horses." She gestures to the new stuffed animal Scarlett gave me. I mean, horses are cool, I guess. I would like to learn how to ride one like Robin Hood. "Robin, how would you feel if you came to live with us for a bit?"

It sounds nice to be able to leave the orphanage, but I know they're only going to return me later. I've seen it happen to a lot of "troublesome" kids. "You don't want me to go live with you."

Mrs. Friar's face falls. "Why not?"

I'm a little nervous to explain, mostly because Scarlett's in the room and I haven't explained any of this to her, but I also don't want Mrs. Friar to get her hopes up. "I have lots of nightmares, and I scream in my sleep. There's probably other stuff too that's wrong with me. You don't want a kid that's gonna be a bunch of problems."

Mrs. Friar's quick to speak. "Robin, that's okay! We all have problems and we are all working on them. I want you to know that just because things are terrible now doesn't mean it won't get better. We all just have to work on it. And there is no such thing as a bad child, there's only children who need help."

"What kind of help?" The idea of getting help scares me. Mom said she was going to get me "help" and it was a terrible place that was going to kill me, one way or another.

"Like therapy."

"I don't want to go to therapy!" That's what Mom said the place she sent me to has and they almost killed me!

"Ok... what about this? What if we get someone who knows what they're doing to talk with you? So that we can all figure out how to help you with things like your nightmares and whatever else there may be. We can figure out what causes them and do what's best for you so that they go away. How does that sound?"

It sounds better, but I'm still scared that at the end of the day I'm only going to be put back here. "I don't think you really want me. I'm just gonna be causing problems."

"Just give us a chance at least. Alright?"

I guess that's the least I can do. It would be nice to be out of the orphanage for a bit. "Okay. But you have to tell Scarlett your address because I want her to visit."

"That's okay then. How about we all go and talk with the director then and get things sorted out?"

"Okay."

They spend a lot of time in the office. I have to wait around for a while, but the nice thing is that Scarlett stays for as long as she can. When the sky starts to get dark, someone comes in to tell me to pack my things. Once I'm done, I'm brought to the office and someone explains that I'm going to go live with Mr. and Mrs. Friar for a while.

With everything done, the three of us walk out of the orphanage and into the parking lot, which feels kinda weird. I've spent a few weeks there, and I thought I was going to be in there for a while. Longer than a few weeks.

We all get in the car, and then Mr. Friar starts driving us to my possibly new home. I just lean my head against the window and look up at the night sky.

"Is there any music you would like to listen to?" Mrs. Friar turns around to ask me.

There's not any music I really like. We didn't really listen to music much, growing up. Just whatever hymns we were singing that Sunday, and I don't really want to hear those anymore. Other than hymns, do I know any other songs?

"Robin?"

Looking at the stars, I have a bit of an answer. "Can we listen to Green Day?"

Mrs. Friar's quiet, a little surprised by my request. I somewhat expect her to say no and that they're too much to listen to, but she just says, "sure."

After a minute, my dad's favorite band begins to play. I recognize "American Idiot", but after that, it's songs I don't know, but they're the most wonderful songs.

There's one song in particular I really like. It's sad, and it's something along the lines of sleeping through September because it's too sad a month.

I never thought a sad song could make me feel better.

Chapter 26

Robin

We slowly roll up to a house that has a few trees in the front yard. I can't tell much about the house itself because of how dark it is, but I know we're a little ways away from town, and in the distance I can make out a stable.

"Alright, we're here," Mrs. Friar tells me. She and her husband get out of the car. I grab my bag and follow.

As we walk into the house, Mrs. Friar puts her arm around me. I know it's meant to be a nice gesture, but feeling her arm makes me uncomfortable. I feel a shiver go up my spine; it feels like her arm's leaving the sticky goo on me that would never come off. The way it seems to fester and bubble makes me want to shove her, but I don't want to be rude. If they're trying to take me in, I should be on my best behavior.

When we go inside, the tour begins. They bring me through every room of the house, saying, "that's the kitchen" and, "that's the living room" and, "that's the bathroom." The house itself seems fairly nice. What doesn't seem super nice is Mrs. Friar talking about how there's gonna be rules about the TV and video games, and how I'm not allowed to touch the record player until they show me how to properly use it.

The tour ends in a bedroom. The room itself is very bland. There's nothing in it except a bookshelf, a bed, and a nightstand. Even then, the bed just has some gray sheets on it.

"This is going to be your room," Mrs. Friar tells me. "I know it doesn't look like much right now, but tomorrow we'll go out and get you some things to decorate it. Does that sound good?"

I nod.

"Alright then. How about you put your stuff down on the bed and then we'll make some dinner?"

"Okay."

Mr. and Mrs. Friar walk to the kitchen, leaving me alone in my room. I'm glad to be alone for once. Don't get me wrong, they seem like nice people, but everything feels like a dream. I'm suddenly thrown into this new home and a whole new family and I just have to act like they're my parents? I don't want new parents. Especially not a new dad. I don't want to ever replace Dad! How can I go through all of that and see how much my dad's sacrificed and then turn around and possibly call this new man—who I've never met before—my father? Or call this new woman—who I just met today—my mother? She might be better than Mom, but am I just supposed to ignore everything that's happened to me the past eleven years? I don't think I can ignore all of that, and everything's happening so fast. I don't know how I feel about any of it.

Do I feel anything about all of it?

"Robin?" someone quietly calls from the door. I turn around to find Mr. Friar by the door. "You ready for dinner?"

I don't really feel hungry, but I know I should eat. "Sure." I put my bag by my bed and then walk with Mr. Friar to the kitchen.

***

By the next morning, all my effort towards making a good impression has failed.

When I wake up, my wrist is hurting really badly and is all sorts of colors. Mrs. Friar takes me to the doctor, and that's how I find out that I had another tantrum in my sleep last night. Apparently aside from screaming, I also fling my body around, which is how I sprained my wrist.

The doctor helps wrap it up and tells Mrs. Friar that I should probably see a sleep specialist and do a sleep study, especially since it's been reported that I'm having them pretty often. He gives her a few things that she can do in the meantime to help either lessen or stop them.

Walking out of the doctor's office, I tell Mrs. Friar, "I'm sorry."

I expect her to make some remark about how I woke her up last night or how I'm gonna be more trouble than I'm worth. Instead she tells me, "it's okay. It happens." She puts a hand on my shoulder, which makes me flinch. I wasn't expecting her to notice it. "You good?"

I really just want to say I'm fine because I know she's going to be hurt about the truth, but at the same time, I don't know if I can deal with all of the touching anymore.

"Robin, you can tell me anything. If it's something you need, I'll do it, no questions asked."

People always say that, and then the second you voice your feelings, they go off on you.

"Robin, tell me what's wrong. Now."

I still don't want to tell her, but she clearly isn't going to let go of the topic. I just let out a sigh and brace for impact. "I don't like it when you touch me."

"Like, at all?"

I nod. Every time she touches me it feels like she's forcing onto me the idea that she's my new mom and that I'm supposed to just move on from everything. Some parts of it I want to move on from, other parts I don't, but either way I can't get myself to move as fast as everyone wants me to.

Mrs. Friar's a little taken aback, but she takes her hand away. "Okay. I won't touch you unless you say so."

I doubt I'll want any contact.

"Does that work for you?"

It does. I nod since I can't get myself to speak.

"Good. Now, you ready to go to the store to decorate your new room?"

That does sound exciting. Especially because I never got to decorate my own room back home. I can't wait to finally have a place I can retreat to that feels like me. "I'm ready."

"Alright." Without holding hands, we walk back to the car and head our way to the store.

Chapter 27

Robin

obin!" Mr. Friar's voice fills the house as he leans his head in from the back door. "Would you mind helping me with something in the field?"

"Like what?"

"I just need some help fixing a fence is all."

Even though it kind of sounds boring, it's much better than doing homework. "Gimme a sec." I grab my coat and boots, then head out the back door where Mr. Friar is.

It's a little chilly as we walk past the stables and to the fields, but it's not anything to complain about. The sun is still shining, but it's definitely going to set soon. Its final rays are trying to reach as far as they can before going to bed for the night.

"The broken one is in that corner over there." Mr. Friar points to it as we're coming up on it. Considering that all I see is a small pile of cracked wood on the ground where a fence is supposed to be, I would consider that broken.

"How are we gonna fix it?"

"I got all the materials we need right there. Just need some help assembling it. We're basically just making a new fence in that portion."

"Cool."

When we get to the fence, the first thing we do is collect all the broken wood and move it away from our little construction site. That doesn't take too long, so it's now time to build it.

"Alright, Robin, so how it works is that this piece of wood, which is called a rail, is going to go in-between these two posts, and we're going to do that by putting each end of the rail into these holes in the post." He points out two holes in the posts that are parallel to each other, but looking at the rail, it seems a little too big to actually fit in.

"Are you sure this is going to work?"

"Yeah. It's all supposed to fit. What I need you to do is take the rail and put it in that post's hole, and I'll guide it into the corner post."

I'm still a little suspicious, but the least I can do is just go along with it. "Okay."

Mr. Friar hands me a rail, which I start sliding into the hole of the first post. "Now, on the count of three, I'm gonna pull this post a bit so there's enough space to get it in, and you're gonna put it in. Got it?"

I nod.

"Alright. One, two, three!"

As Mr. Friar makes enough room for the rail to be put in, I shove the rail into one spot, and then the other. Just like that, it's all in place.

"Hey, good job! Looks great." Mr. Friar smiles as he inspects our work. It grows more and more as he looks at it, which makes me smile a bit. "Now, we've got to do a few more of these. You ready?"

"Yeah." I want to do this whole fence!

It's only a few more rails we have to put in, but it's so much fun. I'm such a man, building and fixing a fence. Getting into the nitty gritty of it all and lifting and carrying things around. It's also nice that Mr. Friar is so happy and proud of me every time we get a rail in place.

"And that's that." Mr. Friar gives the brand new fence a good pat with a grin. "Some of the finest fence making I've seen."

"Really?"

"Really. You did good, kiddo." He gives me a high five, and it makes me so happy. Here I am, learning how to be a man and do manly things with... Mr. Friar.

I wanted to do those things with Dad.

I wanted to learn how to be a man with Dad, not Mr. Friar. I mean, I know that I can't do those things with Dad because he's gone, but I don't want Mr. Friar to take his place. He's not my dad! I don't want him to be my dad!

"Now come on, let's get back in the house. You still got some homework to do."

"No!" I'm not gonna listen to him! Why should I listen to him? Before he can even try to treat me like he's known me all my life, I run away from him and into the trees nearby. I don't want him to try and talk to me or calm me down or whatever. It's all dumb and he doesn't understand anything!

I mean, how can you take in a kid and just act like he's always been in your life? I'm a complete and utter stranger to you, and you're just acting like everything's great and perfect and always has been. You act like I'm supposed to have lived this way my entire life. To a point, it does feel like that. Even though I was in a court case then thrown in an orphanage a month ago, it feels like a lifetime ago; but I had a completely different life before landing in their arms, and they're completely ignoring that! I had a Dad that loved me and did everything for me, and now I'm just supposed to ignore and forget him and act like Mr. Friar is my dad? And Mrs. Friar is my mom?

Mr. Friar tries to call me back, and when I don't come, I hear his footsteps follow me into the woods. I don't stop running until he loses my trail. Once I know I'm far enough and that he can't find me, I take a moment to rest.

I sit by the trunk of a tree and just want to cry and punch something. Why are they so insistent? They're in my face so much and always acting so happy and cheerful. I'm being forced into this perfect picture and I hate it. Everything's not alright! Everything's so messed up! And it's all moving so fast and I'm just supposed to act like my entire life didn't flip itself upside down and completely change? I'm with an entirely different family in a different country, and I'm starting to feel like I'm crazy and I'm the only one that remembers having a past life that no one else can recall or that everyone chooses to forget and doesn't tell me.

The sun disappears pretty quickly, but I want to stay out just a little longer. It's nice to enjoy the cold and the darkness for a moment. It reminds me of Dad, and the last night I had with him. Just walking in the open nature in the dark and the cold and just having fun with him and Scarlett. That last day was so much fun; he had so much joy and energy.

I wish I got more days with him like that. He was like a different person, but in a good way.

After a while, I decide I'm calm enough to go home. I don't feel like punching something anymore, so I think that's calm enough. I know that I'm gonna get questioned, which sucks, but if I don't go now, they're going to start worrying. That, and I still have homework to do.

I start walking to where I think the ranch and the house is, but after walking for a minute, I don't see the field. That's... that's not good. But maybe instead if I walk in this direction for a while, then I'll hit the field. I know how to get out of here, I've been here before. I probably just got a little disoriented.

After walking a different way for a few minutes, the field never comes, and it starts to seep in that I might be lost. I want to look to the north star, but there's so many branches and leaves above me that I can't see the sky.

How am I gonna get out? How long am I gonna be here? Am I gonna be stuck all night? I don't want to be out here anymore. I want to be back inside the house and in bed. Oh, dang it, I still have homework, too! It's already getting late, and I don't know what time it is.

"Robin?" someone shouts from afar.

Just hearing someone's voice makes me jump, and I start looking around. Unfortunately, the woods still look the same.

"Robin?" It's a little louder this time. I turn around, beginning to see a light coming toward me.

"I'm here! Over here!" I cry out. I'm so glad that someone's here. I don't have to be lost anymore.

As whoever it is gets closer, I can hear the horse's hooves galloping. Slowly, not only can I see the horse better, but I can see who's riding it as well. As he comes up to me, I feel very conflicted about it being Mr. Friar. I'm thankful that he's here to take me back to the house, but of all the people to find me I don't want it to be him. Last time we talked didn't end well, and I'm not just gonna forgive him for what he did.

"Oh, Robin, thank god you're alive!" He gets off the horse and runs over to me. "Are you okay?"

"No! Why would I be?" Just like everything else, he decides to forget what happened earlier. That's all he and Mrs. Friar do. They choose to ignore anything about my past or theirs and act like it's always been this way, but it hasn't!

"What's wrong?"

"You! That's what's wrong! You can't just act like there wasn't this whole different life before me."

"What do you mean?"

"I am not your kid! You guys didn't give birth to me! And you're especially not my dad!"

Mr. Friar's face falls a bit when I say that, but I don't care. I mean it, and I'm tired of them acting like it's all okay. "Is that what this is about?"

"What else would it be about?" How can he be so blind to it all? His life changed as suddenly as mine did, yet he looks past that. Just like how one day I have a completely different "family," one day he has this kid that he needs to take care of.

Mr. Friar's quiet for a while. The wind brushing the leaves of the trees is the only thing that fills the silence. "I'm sorry. I... I didn't mean to be your new dad, I just want to give you the best I can."

"Well, can you not?"

"I'll do what you need, Robin. What's your need right now? Do you need an explanation? Or do you want to explain something?"

He gets down to my eye level, and the way that he's acting so calm makes me less angry. I kind of hate that it does because now I don't want to talk, even if he's right that it would help.

I don't know how, but I think he could tell that I can't really speak. "How about this: what did you mean by a whole different life before?"

I know that I should tell him, but the words are somehow buried below the ground. They're also causing so much pain inside my chest. I know it will stop if I get them out, but I just can't. It all hurts so much.

"Was it very different than right now? Is everything going too fast?"

As I start crying, I nod.

"Do we need to slow down for a little while?"

Yeah. I need everything to slow down. I nod again.

"Okay then. We'll take it step by step then. And I'll make sure that Mrs. Friar knows too once we get back home." Mr. Friar gives me a smile. It's very soft; only existing to try and make me feel better. It kind of does. "Can I give you a hug?"

As much as a hug sounds comforting, I don't really want one from Mr. Friar. I would rather have one from Dad. I shake my head.

"Alright. Now, let's get on home. It's late, and you still have school tomorrow."

Right. And I still have homework to do.

Mr. Friar helps me up onto the horse, then gets on behind me. As he holds on to me for my safety, we gallop out of the woods and onto home. It's so relieving to get out of there and see the night sky.

"Before you," Mr. Friar speaks up, out of the blue, "Mrs. Friar and I have been married for a long time. We tried starting a family on our own, but it just wasn't gonna happen for us. She might seem like a tough and stubborn lady, but it really broke her heart. After a period of crying and mourning possibilities, she wanted to adopt, which led us to you. We worked hard and had to wait a bit to get to the point of fostering you, but by the time we met, we were ready for you. We were excited for you, if anything.

"Then again, even if we were ready, that doesn't mean you were ready. That's probably why we've made it feel so fast."

He's not wrong. All that I've gone through since Dad died, I've not been ready for. I wasn't ready to watch my dad die. And I wasn't ready to be thrown in jail or go to court or to be thrown in a home with random strangers that I'm told are my "foster parents" but they won't admit to me that I should just accept that they're my "actual parents" now.

"From now on, we'll go at your pace. Okay? And if I or Mrs. Friar are overstepping, you have full permission to give the word and we won't hold it against you or scold you or whatever. We just want you to have everything you need and that you're comfortable and happy."

That sounds nice. I hope they follow through with it because that kind of life sounds so much less stressful. I just want a moment to breathe. And thinking about how both Mr. and Mrs. Friar respect my space, I think they will do what they say. They haven't really given me reason to doubt their word.

When we get back to the house, Mr. Friar tells me to get ready for bed and not care about whatever schoolwork I had left. I'm nervous, but he promises to email my teacher and explain that there was an emergency that left me unable to do my work. As I put on my pajamas and brush my teeth, I hear him and Mrs. Friar talking. I only catch snippets of the conversation, but I can tell he's doing what he told me he would do.

Once I'm all ready for bed, I get cozy under the covers. Almost immediately, I start drifting off to sleep. But I think at some point, Mr. Friar comes in and says, "goodnight, Robin. I love you." I'm not sure if that's real or a dream, though.

Chapter 28

Robin

Today's my first day of therapy, which I'm not excited about, but it doesn't end up being that bad. Unlike the counselors at that camp Mom sent me to, she doesn't yell or touch me or tell me I'm wrong. I actually sit in my own chair and she sits in hers, and we just talk. She asks me questions, but only tells me to answer if I'm comfortable with it. It's a nice change of pace, and it's kinda relaxing.

But the best part of it all is that Mrs. Friar promised me a present after my first session because she knows that I'm not all that keen about it. I have no idea what the gift is, but when I see Scarlett waiting on the porch, I'm overjoyed.

The second the car is parked, I open the door and run to her. "Scarlett!" I make sure to give her the biggest and tightest hug. I haven't seen her in a few days because of her job. I miss her so much.

She hugs me back. "Hey, how's your day been?"

"It's been interesting." I don't know if I can say it's been good or bad. It's been different, but that's it. "Do you want to come in and play some video games with me?"

"Sure, but Mrs. Friar told me to come over for a specific reason."

"What reason?" This has to do with my present; I know it.

"Robin, Scarlett, come help me unload groceries from the car," Mrs. Friar calls out to us. I get there as fast as I can so I can find out what awesome thing is going on. And so I can carry things and show that I'm a strong man.

Once all the food has been put away, Mrs. Friar brings me to the dining table. Her laptop's on it, which isn't surprising, but what is surprising is that Scarlett's using it. Usually, the laptop is only for the Friars to use because it has a lot of business stuff on it.

"Now, Robin," Mrs. Friar begins, "I know that you're trans, and there's a lot of things I don't know about that topic, but I know there's a lot of things you need. And I do want you to know that I have been calling around to gender clinics and seeing if they're open and what we need to do to get you through to those."

"Does that mean I might get boy hormones soon?" That would be awesome!

"I believe you would just have puberty blockers for a while. But in the meantime, there are other things we can do, and that's what Scarlett is here for."

"What other things?"

"Well," Scarlett starts, "there are two things you can do. You can bind and you can pack. Binding is when you flatten your chest so you look like a boy. You can use a binder or binding tape, but most people use binders. And packing is when you put something down by your crotch so it looks like you have a penis."

"Is that the boy part?"

"Yeah."

Then that sounds awesome. "How do you know all this?"

"I had some trans friends and neighbors growing up, so I've learned a lot about this stuff. That's why Mrs. Friar asked me to help."

"That, and it's always nice to have you around," Mrs. Friar says, which makes Scarlett roll her eyes. "You guys start looking. I'm gonna put a record on."

"Okay."

We look at a few websites that Scarlett has pulled up on the laptop. It's one specific brand that she's heard a lot of people love. We look at a lot of different binders, and there are quite a few I like. They mostly look like bras, but Scarlett assures me that they would flatten my chest. After maybe a half-hour of looking at everything, I decide on one that looks like my skin color, so it won't stick out too much, and a longer one that's white so I can get away with calling it a tank top and no one would question it. I want to get more, but Mrs. Friar says we'll start with two and get more later if I like these ones.

The only thing that sucks is that I have to measure myself, and I have to measure my chest. It's not the worst dysphoria I've felt, but I'm not comfortable. I have to remind myself that it's for binders, which makes me feel a lot better.

Then we talk about packers. There are different kinds of packers, and it can go from using a random sock you have to actually having something that looks like a penis. Some are kinda just for looks, and there are others that you can actually use to pee, which is crazy. Also, penises kinda look weird. But I still want to have one, or something like it.

We have to call Mr. Friar to help with the packers to figure out what would be a good size for me. Once we figure out what size would be good to start, we order one that I can use to pee that is just barely the right size. We have to order some other stuff too so that when I wear it it stays in place and won't look weird, but I don't care as long as I get to look like a boy.

I can't wait for all of it to come!

***

It takes a little while for the packages to get here, but they somehow come on the same day. I get home from school—which was a bit of a rough day—to find the packages on the doorstep. I immediately pick them up and hurry inside.

"Mrs. Friar, they came!" I don't know if she's in the house, but I scream anyway in case she's here.

"What came?" Mr. Friar's voice comes from the kitchen. I think he's doing dishes.

"My binders and packer!" I bring the boxes to the table and toss my backpack on the couch. "Can I open the boxes? Can I try them on?"

Mr. Friar smiles as he chuckles a bit. "Yeah. It's not like you're gonna wait anyway. Let me dry my hands and grab some scissors."

I have to wait a minute, which sucks, but eventually Mr. Friar joins me at the table and opens up the boxes.

The first box is my binders, and once I see them, I get so excited. I start jumping up and down from how happy I am, and once Mr. Friar puts the scissors down, I grab one of them and book it to my room so I can try it on.

After closing the door, I take off my shirt and my dumb bra. With that out of the way, it's just me and the binder. It looks a little small, but I check the label, and it's the size we ordered, so it should fit me.

I pick it up and start trying to put it on. I do well for two seconds. I try to be so delicate putting it on, but I get my arms stuck and can't figure out how to get it on further.

It takes a few more tries, mostly because I'm nervous that it will rip or that it will be too small, but after a few minutes, I get it on. It feels a little tight, but not super tight. It feels really good, especially as I look down at myself and how flat I am.

"Robin." There's a knock on my door, no doubt from Mr. Friar. "Robin, I know you're excited, but you need to come out. We need to make sure it's okay and go over some rules."

Why does there have to be rules about binders?

I open my door and come out of my room anyway, but only so I can go into the bathroom and look at myself with the binder on. I do look pretty flat, like I don't have breasts at all. That's actually insane. This is amazing! Even when you look at me from the side, you wouldn't know!

"How does it feel? Not too tight?" Mr. Friar asks as he looks at me. I'm too busy flexing my muscles in the mirror. That's a real man looking at me.

"Feels fine."

"You sure? You're not just saying that?"

I groan. Why would I lie? "I'm sure."

"Alright. It looks pretty fine. Now remember, Scarlett said that you can't wear it for more than eight hours. You can wear it to school, and you can wear it out and about, but if you're home or it's been more than eight hours, it's off. Got it?"

"Got it." I don't like the idea, but I know it's because they don't want my ribs to get destroyed from wearing it too much.

"And no wearing it while you sleep."

"I won't." I throw my shirt on so I can see what it looks like if I'm at school or walking around. You can see the straps a bit, but if it's the nude one or the white one, I can get away with it pretty well. "Can we open the packer stuff too?"

"Sure, but don't go running off this time."

"Fine."

We both go back to the kitchen, and Mr. Friar opens the other box. This time, though, he makes sure to hold me back so I can't grab it and start messing with it. When he pulls the packer and stuff out, it takes all of my being to not try and grab it out of his hands.

"Okay, Robin, every day that you use this, you need to wash it at the end of the day. Marilyn and I can help you the first few times, but after that we want you to take care of it."

"Is it complicated to wash?"

"No, but we just want to make sure that you know how to clean it the right way."

"Okay. Can I put it on now? Can I try peeing with it?"

"You can *try*, but make sure to see if it feels comfortable."

"Yeah, okay! Thanks!" I grab the packer and the jockstrap for it and run to the bathroom.

I close the door and quickly get the jockstrap and the packer on. It's absolutely perfect. The jockstrap actually helps a lot and keeps the packer in place, and it feels very comfortable. It's so different to look down and see a penis. It feels different too, but I know I'll get used to it. I feel like a true man with it on. Just wearing the packer makes me so happy that I want to run around the bathroom. I feel like I can fly with how joyful I am, but I know better than to try that.

"Robin, make sure to practice in the shower please," I hear Mr. Friar's voice say. I think it's dumb, because it can't be that hard to pee into the toilet with this thing. Cis guys do it all the time ever since they were like, two. You just got to aim and pee.

Still, I step into the shower and get ready to pee standing up for the first time. I've been waiting a while to do this. I'm gonna be such a man! I can't believe I'm actually going to do this!

I don't know how this happens, but as much as some of the pee comes out the way it's supposed to, a lot of it... doesn't.

How did I pee all over myself? Now my pants are all wet! And the jockstrap too. Oh, come on!

What do I do now? I don't want to go out there with wet pants. It's so embarrassing, even if it's just Mr. Friar out there.

"Robin, you good in there?"

"Yeah," I lie. But I really need new pants... "I am doing amazing, but can you get a pair of pants from my room? Just because I want to wear different pants, no other reason." I hope that's enough for him to not catch on.

"There's a pair right by the door."

That was rather quick.

I pop a hand out from the bathroom and grab the new pair of pants. After using a bunch of toilet paper to dry myself off, I put the clean pair of pants on. The jock strap is still a little damp, but I can't do much else about that, and I'm not about to just take my packer off because of some mishap.

Once I'm all dressed, I quickly book it for my room and throw the dirty pair of pants in the hamper, then walk out to the living room acting like I didn't screw up peeing, because I totally didn't.

I walk over to where Mr. Friar is, acting all cool. I mean, beside the little accident in the bathroom, I feel over the moon about the packer.

He's sipping on some coffee as I come in. When he sees me, he asks, "All good?"

I nod. "The goodest."

"Good to hear." He takes another sip. "Now, you ready to go out?"

"Yeah." I get ready and then head outside with Mr. Friar. He promised me that he would teach me how to ride a horse today.

Chapter 29

Robin

kay, class, let's put our books away because it's time for current events," Ms. Castleton tells us. I don't really want to put my book down, but I know that just ignoring everything and continuing to read would end up with me having to sit out in the hall, so I put it down.

The papers start being passed around, and eventually they get around to my table. One of my classmates hands one to me, and I take a look at it.

New Canadian law passed protecting Queer American refugees!

I can already feel my chest tensing up. I don't think this is going to go well for me.

"Alright, everyone, I'll let you take a moment to read it, then we'll discuss it as a class."

Thank god for that. I don't know if I can handle having to read it aloud or hearing my other classmates read about something I've had to deal with. Hopefully reading it isn't gonna be too much of a problem.

Richard Lea has much to celebrate today, as his proposition to change laws surrounding refugees, particularly queer minors, including those from the United States, has passed.

It feels weird to see a photo of the man who represented me in court in my classroom. Just reading the article makes me feel nauseous.

Lea was originally inspired to work toward this amendment after working a refugee case that captured the minds and hearts of the Canadian public that surrounded a young transgender boy who had escaped the United States shortly after the country passed its laws encouraging the destruction of American LGBTQ+ citizens.

Are... Are they talking about me? Am I the transgender boy?

The story of John Doe grasped the attention of the world as many wondered about his fate considering his deceased father and his mother who lives back in America, but had neglected Doe's health needs as a transgender child. With the wonderful work done by Lea, the child was both accepted into Canada and protected from extradition back to the United States, and, according to Lea, is now in a safe and loving home.

"Young Doe was not the only child that has gone through this and will not be the only child going through this process," Lea told us in an exclusive interview. "The changes are so that we have a system in place for the many future queer kids that come to our country for their safety. With the new laws in America, there will be an influx of immigrants and refugees, both adults and children, whether we want it or not."

I feel like I'm gonna throw up.

"Alright class, let's talk about this. What are your initial thoughts?"

One girl raises her hand and is called on. "Is the case they're talking about the one that happened a month or so ago?"

"Yes. Does everyone remember the clips that were going around about the boy in court and his testimony?"

Everyone nods but me.

"That's the same boy that's being referenced in the article."

Wait... there's videos of my case out there? What do they look like? What are the videos of exactly? Me having to talk in court? The video Mr. Lea made me do so I didn't have to give my full testimony? Does that mean that everyone's seen me cry? Do they know what I look like? How much do they know about me because of the video?

Ms. Castleton calls on another classmate whose hand is up. "I thought America was the country that was all about freedom. Why can't transgender and queer people live in America anymore?"

"That is a great question, Rocky. You see, the United States has been passing laws recently that lets them hurt people who are part of the LGBTQ community."

"But America's supposed to be welcoming to everyone." You can tell the kid is really confused. So are a lot of my other classmates. They can't understand the contradictions of those words, let alone living in that kind of world.

"They say a lot of things like that, but they are what we call hypocrites. They say one thing, but then don't follow through with it. Does that make sense?"

The kid shakes his head, as if it's impossible for someone to not follow through on their word.

"Henry," Ms. Castleton points out, "I see you have your hand raised."

"Okay, so like I know that they're called transgender people and whatever, but I heard that in America they're called predators. Why are they called different things?"

"Ms. Castleton!" I cry out while trying to make sure the vomit doesn't get past my throat. "I don't feel very well."

"Do you need to go to the nurse?"

I nod.

"Alright. Marian, do you mind helping Robin to the nurse's office?"

She agrees, so we both get up and Marian helps me get there. Even though I feel better by the time we're at the office, I decide to stay in there till my class is done with the article.

***

At recess, I'm playing kickball with all my classmates. I'm doing pretty good. I got a double and a home run so far, so it's safe to say that I'm going to get picked first next time we have to pick teams. I take great pride in that.

I'm waiting for my turn to be the kicker. I think I'm a few people away, but what's annoying is that Henry's behind me. Even before today, he really bothered me. He always says really weird things. I don't think a lot of kids like him, but it's not like he's *really* a pain. Just annoying and weird in a creepy way.

Even right now as he's talking to one of his friends, some of the things he's saying is really pissing me off. "That article Ms. Castleton made us read was weird."

"Super weird," his friend agrees. I think all his friends just agree with what he says.

"I wanted to say more in class, but I knew Ms. Castleton wouldn't like what I would've said."

"What were you gonna say?"

"Transgender people are creeps. Imagine not knowing who you are and confusing your gender in the process. How dumb do you have to be to do that?"

"Hey, Henry." I turn around because I can't help it, but I try really hard to keep my fist from going above my waist. "Shut up. Please." I add the *please* so I can at least say that I was polite in doing it.

"What? I'm just saying. Maybe America's right. Most of those people are crazy for their entire lives. You can't have a healthy nation with crazy people."

I'm not crazy! What the hell is he saying?

"Henry, remember that one American guy? The one that kidnapped his daughter and they caught him trying to get to Canada? I bet he was one of those crazies too."

"Why else would he have been running to Canada? Not only was he crazy, but I heard his daughter was crazy. She was one of those kids who thought she was transgender."

"Really?"

"Yeah. Her dad molested her and because of that she thought she was a boy or something. It's a shame that they didn't kill the daughter, but thank god they got him. My dad said that all the Richard Wrights of the world deserve that death, he was genuinely insane!"

"Fuck you!" I slam my fist into Henry's disgusting mouth to make him shut up. He doesn't know shit! My dad wasn't insane or disturbed or whatever other things he's said, and he doesn't get to ruin my father's name!

"What the hell?" Henry spits, a little blood flying out of his mouth. "Oh, you're asking for it!"

He starts punching and kicking me. It hurts pretty bad, but I don't care as long as he comes out worse than me. He needs to learn that queer people are stronger and braver than he could even dream, and that you don't talk bad about the man who saved me and loved me. I throw every single punch I can and make sure to kick him as if he is the ball and I get a home run. Even after five seconds of him attacking me, he's looking a lot bloodier than I. That brings me joy because I'm already showing him who's boss.

I feel someone grab my shoulders and pull me away from Henry. Even though he's getting further and further away, I make sure to make any last kicks or hits I can. Thankfully, I get the last say and my foot connects with his jaw.

"Both of you, to the principal's office!"

Chapter 30

Robin

With a bloody swollen lip and a black eye, I have to sit in the office with all my stuff and wait for Mrs. Friar to come pick me up.

How could the principal take Henry's side? I told her he was saying bad things about queer people and that they should all be killed, but I'm the one who's in trouble because I threw the first punch? That's bullcrap. And now I'm suspended for three days.

Mrs. Friar is not going to be happy when she picks me up. I hope she's not gonna be super angry, because if she's angry then I'm gonna get angry and then it's gonna be a mess.

At least Henry is more beat up than me. I hope he learned his lesson.

"Robin?" one of the secretaries calls out. "Your mother's here."

She's not my mom, but whatever.

I grab my backpack and get up. Walking over to the front, I start seeing Mrs. Friar. Her face is so neutral that I can't tell what she's thinking or feeling. It honestly scares me even more than her being angry.

"Thank you," she says to the secretary as her arm goes around my shoulder. It's definitely to monitor where I am, which I hate. It's not like I'm gonna run. Where would I even go?

We walk to the car in the parking lot, Mrs. Friar not saying a single word to me. I get in and buckle up in the backseat as she quietly starts up the car. As we drive by, there's no music playing, and we just sit there in absolute silence. She doesn't look at me in any way. Even though I don't regret the fight per se, I don't like what's happening. I feel like I failed in some way. But I stood up for what I believe in and the people I love, like a real man. Just like Dad taught me.

When we get home, Mrs. Friar immediately brings me inside, and it's only when she's done dragging me to my room, does she say anything. "Robin, I am very disappointed in you."

"You don't get it! He started it!"

"You threw the first punch. Hurting people is wrong and you know that."

"He was calling trans people crazy and talking bad about my dad!"

Mrs. Friar's face finally changes. One of her eyebrows rises. "Explain."

"He was saying that trans people are crazy and dumb and that they should all die because they're not healthy or some shit, but the principal didn't care about any of that!"

"Robin, we do not swear in this household."

"And he said that my dad deserved to die and that he was insane! My dad's none of that!"

I expect Mrs. Friar to say something to cool me down, or how just because people are saying things doesn't mean I should knock some sense into them. Instead, she's rather quiet. Quiet for too long. But it's not like the quiet in the car to make me feel bad. It's a different kind of silence. "How does he know your dad?"

"Everyone knows my dad and everyone talks shit about him when he did the right thing!"

"Robin, let's take a moment to breathe, okay?"

I hate the idea of having to calm down—by breathing no less—but I do as she says and take a few deep breaths with her. And even though I won't admit it to her, I don't feel as hot headed as a minute ago.

"Now, how does everyone know about your dad?"

It kind of surprises me that she hasn't put two and two together. I know she has my birth certificate and stuff, or something like it, but I guess if they're names on a page, maybe they're not as easy to connect. "Do you remember how in January, in America, there was a dad who kidnapped his daughter, and they called him nasty things." I can't really get myself to say what they called him.

She has to think about that, but even after thinking she doesn't come up with much.

"They were from Texas, and the mom was saying a lot of crazy anti-trans stuff."

"Yes, I think it's ringing a bell."

"That was my mom, and he was my dad. And he wasn't any of those things they called him—he loved me and supported me coming out which is why he took me and we ran to Canada!" I cry out. I don't want Mrs. Friar to think that my dad was a bad person like everyone else says. I don't want her to believe the lies.

Mrs. Friar has nothing to say. She just watches as the tears start forming in my eyes. I don't like how I'm crying in front of her, but I can't really hold it in. I'm tired of everyone calling my dad a bad person—I don't understand why everyone does! Is there anyone who will actually try to understand what happened to him and I? I know parts and pieces of it all are separated, and I don't want to be the center of everyone's attention, but can someone just open their eyes and realize that maybe the boy who was in that trial that apparently everyone loves, who talked about how much his dad did for him, is the same boy who was "kidnapped" by his "confused" and "predator" dad? Without Mom finding out back home. Just so everyone can understand that my father, Richard Wright, was actually the most wonderful man and dad in the whole world.

Slowly, Mrs. Friar gets down to my eye level. "If you don't mind me asking, what was your father's name?"

I try to say it, but it gets caught in my throat for a second. I never thought it would be hard to say Dad's name. "Richard Wright."

"I see." She nods, and I expect her to say more about it, but she doesn't. "And this other kid made fun of your dad, as well as you, whether or not he was knowingly doing both of those things, and that's why you punched him?"

I'm a little hesitant, but I nod my head.

"Was it a trigger?"

It's getting a little harder to look at Mrs. Friar, so I focus on my bed sheets as I nod again.

"Is there anything else about it that you want to tell me?"

I don't really want to talk anymore. Talking about Dad makes me feel really sad. Or maybe the word is depressed. My therapist has been saying that word a lot more.

"Robin?"

"I really tried to not punch him. I was doing good until he brought up... brought up you know..."

Mrs. Friar understands what I mean. "Alright then. I'll get you an ice-pack for your eye. You lay here and rest."

I nod and just lay down on my bed. As she's getting the ice, I can hear her on the phone. "Hello, can I speak to the principal? Yeah, I'll hold for a second.

"Hey, I just talked with Robin, and he says that not only did he tell you that he was provoked, but also that you ignored his side of the story."

It's quiet for a moment as I assume the principal's speaking.

"I agree that Robin shouldn't have started the fight, but you're letting the other kid get off scot-free? The kid who said queer people should die? I can forgive you for not knowing that those are very sensitive topics for Robin, but I can't forgive you for absolutely dismissing it. In my opinion, that says a lot about who *you* are as a person, Mrs. Lewis."

I can hear the principal begin to start talking, but Mrs. Friar quickly shuts her down. "As a guardian of a child attending your school, it is extremely concerning because then I can't help but wonder how you would treat disputes about the same topics, or even treat kids who are transgender. Or even kids of different races. And before you even dare utter it, I can assure you there are queer children who are within your school walls—and no, they're not confused.

"But of course, that wouldn't appear to be the case if you punish the kid for what he said. Is what he said not at all concerning to you?"

I'm expecting Mrs. Friar to come in with the ice-pack any moment now, but I haven't heard her move. That, and I'm getting a little nervous where the call is going. I've met Mrs. Lewis numerous times since I "get in trouble a lot." A lot more than Mrs. Friar knows. I've gotten to know her well because she's suspicious about my accommodations and is sure that I'm "faking the trauma and diagnosis so I can get extra time on tests."

"Well then," Mrs. Friar speaks after a while, "you seem to be very stuck on your point, and I'm very stuck on mine. Thankfully, I'm stuck on concrete while you're stuck on straw, so we'll see who lasts the fire."

Oh no. She's in trouble.

Mrs. Friar casually walks into my room, holding the ice pack I'm waiting for. She gently puts it on my eye as she starts dialing on her phone. "Here's the ice for you."

"Thank you," I make sure to say, mostly because I know that I should be on her good side. I'm still a little curious where this is going, though. "What are you doing?"

"Oh, I'm just getting your principal fired, that's all," she says, a little smile on her face as she looks at me. "I love you, Robin."

The way she's acting so casual about it makes me laugh. I smile a little bit back as I hold the ice-pack in place.

Mrs. Friar's kinda done a lot for me. And she still is. I feel a little bad because I've been blind about a lot of it. But she did get me a bunch of new clothes, and binders and packers, and she let me choose what to decorate my room with, and got me books. And she welcomes Scarlett every time she comes by, and is now getting the worst principal ever fired.

As her phone rings, Mrs. Friar asks me, "can I give you a hug?"

Even though I still feel a bit of hesitancy, I kinda want one. "Yeah."

She puts her arm around me and gives me a little squeeze. I don't know why, but that makes me feel really happy. For the first time in a long while, I feel safe and comforted by someone's embrace.

Chapter 31

Robin

hen the doorbell rings, I leap out of my chair and find Scarlett behind the door. I give her a big hug. It might've been a little too strong because she stumbles back a bit.

She laughs. "Hey, Robin."

"Hey. How have you been doing?"

"Good. Though it's too quiet over there."

"I can imagine. I mean, who's gonna make all the noise if you're by yourself? Now, come on inside!"

Scarlett comes on in and closes the door behind her. We go to the living room and play some Mario Kart while Mr. and Mrs. Friar finish making dinner. I'm so excited because this time I think I'm finally gonna beat her. I've been practicing all week.

So you can imagine my disappointment when she still gets first.

"Come on!"

"Nice try." Scarlett smirks.

"Alright, rematch."

"If you insist. It ain't going to change the results."

"Oh, it will." All that practice can't go to waste!

We do another round of races, and it gets close at times, but I'm barely able to squeeze by and get first place. I do just one point better than Scarlett.

After screaming and jumping with joy, I take a moment, and then turn toward Scarlett while trying to act calm and cool. Now it's my turn to smirk. "Well, would ya look at that. I won."

"You threw a red shell at me right at the end!"

"And? Last I checked, that's part of the game."

"I'm just saying, if you didn't get it as your last item you wouldn't have won. You just got lucky."

"You're just jealous." I laugh to myself a bit.

"We just need to play another round."

"That's something a jealous person would say."

Before Scarlett can say anything, Mrs. Friar's voice calls out from the kitchen. "Robin! Scarlett! Time for dinner!"

I run to the kitchen. Unfortunately, Scarlett's really fast, and by the time I get to the kitchen, she catches up to me. And once she does, she puts me in a headlock. "Say it was a lucky shot! Come on. No way you beat me through skill."

"I won it fair and square!"

"But using that red shell right at the end was a dirty move."

"Kids!" Mrs. Friar's voice reigns. "Behave and sit at the table."

"I ain't your kid," Scarlett points out.

"You're under *my* roof."

Scarlett rolls her eyes, but is smiling and chuckling a bit as she lets go of me. The two of us sit down as Mr. and Mrs. Friar place the food on the table. Once everything is ready, they join us.

Before we can start grabbing our food, Mrs. Friar begins talking. "Robin, we have some possible news for you."

I get a little nervous, my heart starting to pound a little harder against my chest. "What is it?"

A little smile grows on Scarlett's face as Mrs. Friar takes a breath. "You've lived with us for a little while now, and it's had its ups and downs, but we've gotten through it."

"Yeah." I'm very glad that I got placed with the Friars. They've been a little stern, but so nice; they've looked out for me. I feel very lucky that, of all the foster parents to have picked me, it was them. Especially because Dad didn't have great experiences. I sometimes wonder if somehow in heaven, he sent them to pick me.

"We've had our troubles, and we've had our joys, and while it feels like it's been a long time being together as a family, I know that for you it feels very different. So tonight we wanted to ask you, how would you feel about us officially adopting you?"

I'm so surprised to hear those words. I mean, at this point, I don't think they would try to return me. Mrs. Friar has put a lot of love, effort, and work into me. She's helping me transition more and feel comfortable, and she's also getting me therapy and helps me understand more things about myself than I thought I knew, and she's always stood up for me when it comes to things I need, whether that be in school or somewhere else.

"You can say no if you want to. You have no need to agree."

I know that. I would never be forced to say yes to being adopted. And I know that I'm not going to go anywhere else, and I don't really want to go anywhere else. I like it here. I just don't know... There's a lot that comes with that. "Would I have to call you guys mom and dad?" I don't want to call Mrs. Friar "mom" because I had a terrible mom. And I don't want to call Mr. Friar "dad" because I don't want to forget Dad.

"You don't have to if you don't want to. Or we could come up with different things you can call us, or even just calling us by our first names."

That makes me feel better, but there's another thing that concerns me. "Would I have to change my name?"

"Don't you want to change your name?"

"Not my last name. I still want to be a Wright. No offense."

"And we don't take any offense to that. If you want to keep your last name, you can happily keep it. We know that it's very important to you."

That makes me feel better about it all. In that sense, it wouldn't be much different than what life already is. It would just be official, I guess.

"Do you need time to think? You can take as long as you need."

No, I don't think I need time. "I would love to be adopted by you guys."

Everyone at the table grins. Mrs. Friar asks, "are you sure? We don't want to force you or make you rush into a decision."

"Yeah, I'm sure." I smile at her, kicking my feet a bit as I sit in my chair. Seeing her happy makes me happy.

Mr. and Mrs. Friar come over and give me the biggest hugs. Even Scarlett comes over and hugs me. It feels so nice to be surrounded by a bunch of people who love me and actually want to care for me and do what's best for me. I can trust them; they'll always have my back, even if the rest of the world won't.

My new family is like my own band of Merry Men.

"I love you, Robin."

"Love you, kiddo."

"You're the worst," Scarlett remarks.

It only makes me feel a little cocky. "Because I beat you at Mario Kart?"

"Maybe." Scarlett will never admit the truth. "But I love you, too."

She puts up her fist, and I give her a fist bump.

"I'm so glad you want to stay with us," Mrs. Friar tells me. "Mostly because I had already bought you some adoption presents."

"You got presents for me?"

"We need to celebrate somehow! Now, it's not official till all the documents are done, but if you want to go through with it, we'll make sure to get it going."

Mr. Friar leaves the room to go grab the presents. I wonder what they got me. I hope it's something good.

He comes back carrying a really big gift bag. What can be in there that's so big?

"Can I open it now?"

"Go ahead."

I pull out all the tissue paper that's covering the mysterious object. It doesn't take long to find something so glorious and holy.

I can't believe it. There's no way the Friars got this for me. I pull it out of the bag and take a good look at it. It's just what I thought. "An *American Idiot* vinyl?"

"It took a while to find it, but we know how much it means to you. That being said, what's our rule when listening to it?"

"Don't sing the swear words." At least not while they're around. If I'm home alone, it's all fair game.

Mrs. Friar smiles because she thinks I'm following her rules. "That's not the only thing in the bag. Take another look."

I'm a little confused, but gently put the record down. I pull some more tissue paper out of the bag. There's a photo frame in it, which is weird. Why would they want to give me a photo frame?

I pick it up and flip it over so I can see the front. I'm expecting to see the fancy decorated frame that probably has some swirls and twirls on it. But I'm not expecting a photo to be in it already.

And it's a photo of Dad.

I can't tell when the photo was taken. It looks like an older photo, but he's happy and smiling. It reminds me a bit of that last day I had with him before he died. How silly and funny he was, and how he just didn't give a care in the world and was as joyful as could be.

Oh, I've missed seeing just his face.

"Do you like it?"

I can't get any words in my mouth as tears fill my eyes, so I just nod my head.

"I want you to know that we are never going to try and replace your parents."

"Especially your father," Mr. Friar speaks up. "And if I am ever overstepping, let me know."

"I will." I make sure to tell Mr. Friar, for his sake. "But how did you guys get this photo?"

"Well," Mrs. Friar begins, "when you told me who your father was, I did a little research and found a few friends he had when he went to university. They gave me a few photos they had from back then, and this was one of them."

"Can I have the other photos, too?"

"I can get them printed for you." Mrs. Friar smiles at me. Just the thought that she would do that for me makes me grin.

We all eat, and the food is so delicious. It feels more yummy than usual. And the chocolate pie is so good.

When dinner and dessert is done, I play my new record. It sounds a little different than when I hear it in my headphones, but I like it. The fact that I have "American Idiot"—one of Dad's favorite songs —on a vinyl record is amazing. I just listen to the music as I look at the photo of Dad.

It starts getting late, and even though the rock music is blasting, I start to doze off. Mrs. Friar can tell and gently taps my shoulder to tell me it's time for bed. I brush my teeth and get ready while Mrs. Friar gently puts *American Idiot* away with the other records. Once I'm done, I get under the covers of my bed and make myself nice and comfy. Before I doze off, though, I make sure to put the framed photo of my dad on my nightstand. Now, every single night I can sleep with Dad close to me. Just falling asleep tonight and having the ability to see his face makes me so happy.

Mrs. Friar comes into my room after a minute. "Matthew had to go out and find a horse that ran off because the owner left the stall door open, but once he's done he'll come and say goodnight to you."

"Okay."

"I hope you had fun tonight."

"I did, don't worry."

"Good. Well then, sleep well." Mrs. Friar gives me a hug. "Goodnight, Robin. I love you."

A thought pops into my head, and even though it scares me to say it, I think I actually mean it. As Mrs. Friar goes to turn off the lights, I tell her, "love you, too."

Hearing that, she smiles.

She turns off the lights and leaves the room. As the glow-in-the-dark stars on my ceiling start to dimly shine, I look at Dad's photo. I try to enjoy his presence all night, but my eyes slowly begin to droop.

I miss you, Dad. But don't worry about me. I think I'm gonna be okay.

Epilogue

Robin

15 YEARS LATER

’m really scared," little Arlo speaks up from the back of the car as we start inching our way towards the border. "What if they catch us?"

"I've done this thousands of times before. It's all going to be fine." I look toward the back seat, making sure to give my best smile to the kid that's scared out of their mind. I'm the only comfort they can get in this whole new world they've been thrown into. "Now, just sit back and relax. Take a nap if you need to."

"Mr. Robin, I—"

"It's okay. It's okay." I want to give them a hug, so I give them a pat on the leg. "Let me worry about everything."

Arlo's fighting tears in their eyes, but they nod and keep quiet. I won't deny that I'm a little nervous about it too. I'm always a little nervous, but over the years it's definitely gone down. The nerves of passing the border with fake documents is like a pinprick happening for a blood test.

I pull the car up to the gate, and one of the border guards starts going through their regular spiel. It's all going smoothly, and then comes the time that they ask, "can we see identification for the two of you?"

"Yessiree, sir." I pull out a few papers from my backpack, which is in the seat next to me. I show my Canadian license, passport, and then a fake birth certificate for Arlo.

"Robin William Wright?"

"Yes, sir."

The guard looks into the back of the car. "Arlo Dale Wright?"

Thankfully, the kid does as I told them and says, "yes."

The guard doesn't seem pleased with that, though. "Why is he crying?"

"They're just a little homesick from their Mama. That, and we were supposed to arrive a few days earlier but ran into a few problems. They're just scared that we're not gonna get home by Christmas, is all."

"Is that true?" the guard asks them.

As I look over my shoulder, Arlo's trying to regain their breath from all their tears. I hope they can get themself to talk. If not, I'll figure something out. All I can do for now is give them a friendly grin.

Arlo finally is able to say something. "Yeah. I miss Mom a lot. And home. Can we go home?"

"Don't worry, kiddo, we'll be home and safe soon enough." I make sure to sound calm so that Arlo will be as well.

"Well then, I guess everything looks alright. Have a good rest of your day, and Merry Christmas."

"Merry Christmas," I tell the guard. Once I make sure that we get our papers back, I roll up the window and drive forward. And soon enough, we're on the road again. With all of that in the rearview mirror, I smile. Another queer kid saved from murder. Another kid that gets to actually grow up and live their life to the fullest.

It takes a while for Arlo to stop crying. I don't say anything about it. I've been in their position before, and they're like all the other kids. No matter how many times I see it, it's always heartbreaking to pick up the kid that requested help and find a child that's so sick and depressed and desperate to leave the states, which gets worse and worse every year. It's safe to say that they're feeling a lot right now. I'm honestly a little surprised that Arlo spoke up at all. "So am I going to go to the big center everyone goes to? How long until we get there?"

"Usually yes, but it wouldn't really be fun spending Christmas in a random place surrounded by strangers, would it?"

Arlo shakes their head. "It wouldn't."

"I know that you barely know me, but if you want, you can join me and my family for Christmas."

Looking in the mirror, I can see Arlo have the biggest smile spread across their face. I don't think I have ever seen them smile like that this whole time. "Really? I'd love to have Christmas with you!"

"Aww, shucks."

"Who's gonna be there?"

"Well, at the least, my mama and papa, my sister and her wife, and probably their two dogs, and my own wife as well."

"That's a lot of family. I'm excited to meet all of them."

"I'm excited to see 'em, too."

Thankfully, the drive doesn't feel that long to my parents' house. Even though it's dark outside when I roll up to the driveway, there's someone waiting on the porch. Seeing her face again and her bright red jacket makes me jollier than any Christmas song that plays on the radio. Though, the second I turn off the car and open the door, she's immediately heckling me with, "what took you so long, you—"

"Watch your language," I annoyingly point out. It's going to be one of the few times I can get away with it. "I have a kid with me. They're spending Christmas with us, if that's alright."

"First of all, I didn't swear."

"Yet." I'm not going to let Scarlett get out of this one.

"And second, you should've called Mama Marylin before you got here to make sure we had enough room and food."

"Mama's gonna have enough. There's plenty of leftovers every year—what makes this one different?"

Scarlett rolls her eyes as Arlo gets out of the car, but I don't care. The little kid grabs their bag and runs straight for the porch. The first thing they do is go up to Scarlett. "Hello, my name is Arlo. It's really nice to meet you!"

My older sister gives them a grin. "Nice to meet you, too. I'm Scarlett, Robin's sister."

"You're so lucky to have Robin as a brother. He's the coolest, most awesomest person in the whole world. And he's one of the sweetest people ever."

"I wouldn't call him the coolest," Scarlett jokes. "But he's pretty good at what he does. And I would say he's very brave for doing it. It's admirable."

"So is being a lawyer and making sure those kids stay safe," I point out. "I only do half of the work."

"Stop being humble. It's annoying," my sister sneers.

Before I can snap back, I hear a joyful cheer from inside. A minute later, I'm bombarded by Mama. "Oh, Robin, baby, you're home!" She runs over to me and gives me the biggest hug. It makes me chuckle a bit, but Mama is also one of the best huggers. I've missed her hugs, and I always forget until I'm back in one. "Oh, I'm glad you made it home safe. It's so nice to see you."

"Mama, I always get home safe," I try to tell her, but it doesn't matter. She'll always worry about me.

I expect her to start demanding me to help with making Christmas dinner, as she always does, but instead she scowls at me. "You need to shave. You've got too much stubble."

"Oh my god, Mama!"

Scarlett chuckles from where she is.

Mama starts going off. "You can't go around walking like that, especially on Christmas."

"I'm trying to grow it out! It's not gonna look good right now. It will later. Ask Papa, he'll understand."

"Robin, that's a losing battle. Your papa's always been clean-shaven," Mama points out. I love her, but she's really getting on my nerves.

But it's not about dinner, which she usually forces on everyone immediately. Something's up. "Why aren't you bugging me about food?"

Mama sighs as she looks at me with a soft smile. "Well, you're not gonna help us with dinner this year."

"What do you mean by that?"

"Did you not hear?"

"You're such a terrible husband and father." Scarlett smirks at me.

I'm about to make a snarky remark back, but then I actually process what she said. "Wait... the baby was born?"

"Just yesterday morning. It was a nice healthy birth on both ends," Mama assures me.

I'm glad that it went well, but I'm more focused on the baby I haven't met yet. "Where is he? Is he with Marian?"

"They're right upstairs. You go say hi to them," Mama tells me. "I'll help the little kiddo settle in."

"Thank you. I have a present for them in my bag, if you want to wrap that later tonight. Should be in the middle pocket." With that, I walk inside and head upstairs.

I assume our room is the same as last year, so I go into my old bedroom. I make sure to be very gentle when opening the door so I don't freak Marian out. She looks up from what she's doing, and when I walk in, I see she's holding our newborn child.

My gaze meets my wife's, and I smile at her. "You look really beautiful."

"Thank you. You look pretty handsome yourself."

Even after all these years, I find myself blushing at the comment. "I'm sorry I wasn't there when he was born."

"It's alright. You had important things to do. Besides, I had your mother and sister with me."

"I'm glad they could be there for me." I still feel guilty that I missed the birth of my child. That's something I should've been there for, that I was supposed to be there for. As much as Arlo was an emergency and I was all that was available to save them, I wish that I didn't miss something so important. I don't regret saving Arlo at all; it's just unfortunate that the baby came earlier than the due date and that I missed it.

"Would you like to hold him?" Marian asks me as I sit on the bed next to her. I nod, and she gently hands him to me.

My little baby boy's wrapped up in a blanket and has a small beanie on his head. His blue eyes look at me, and he's the cutest thing in the whole world. I hold him close to my chest, and all I can do is smile.

This little baby seems to hold my breath. It takes me a moment to get any words out. "Hi," I say to my son in awe-struck marvel and love. I'm filled with such indescribable joy. I'm so happy, and I feel like I'm going to gush tears of joy just from this tiny living being in my arms. Is this how Dad felt towards me? No wonder he loved me so much and did so much for me. "I'm your dad."

My little boy just stares back at me, in absolute wonder on who this man in front of him is. He seems eased by hearing my voice.

"Is he named—"

"Yes, he is," Marian answers before I can finish asking. She knew what I was going to say. We had talked about it so many times before, and the fact that we got to use that name makes me so happy. Especially because I wasn't there at his birth. My wife gives me a kiss and grins. "How about the two of you spend some time together? I'd really like to take a nap and I bet you would want to be with him."

"Of course. Take as long as you need." I give Marian one more kiss and then get up and leave her alone.

Even though it's cold out, I go outside with my baby. We just stand on the porch together, and I can't help but look at the stars.

I hope Dad's doing well up there.

I look over at my son, seeing his gaze up at the stars. It makes me smile. "See those bright things up there? Those are called stars. They're these bright burning things that are gajillions of miles away. There's many of them, and they all have different names. And that one," I point to a bright star far up in the sky, "is called Polaris. Also known as the North Star. It's called that because it's always going to be north of you."

Little Richard's eyes are stuck on Polaris and how bright it is. I'm glad he likes the stars. I can't wait to teach him everything I know, including the man he's named after.

"I love you, Richie," I tell my baby boy before giving him a little kiss on the forehead.

Acknowledgements

This book has happened so fast but has been one of the most wonderful projects I have done. There is so much raw emotion and love poured into these words and I am nothing short of proud of it.

I would like to give a huge shout-out to Cadence, who not only has been my friend for the longest time, but was a wonderful beta reader that helped me figure things out. I would also like to thank Sarah for being another amazing pair of eyes and helping strengthen the heart of this story in ways that I could not see.

I also want to give a huge thanks to my editor. I will admit that grammar is where I'm weakest, and if it wasn't for her, this novel would be massively hindered by it's flaws.

Aside from the people who have worked on this book with me, I would like to thank Adam for being a consistent pillar of support, whether or not that comes with some sarcasm. I know that there are times where I've been a lot, and I am thankful for every time you were there to help me figure things out.

And though I hate to say it, I wouldn't have this story if it weren't for a strict and traumatic religious upbringing. So, I'll acknowledge that.

About the Author

Artúr Faye is a queer American author. Born and raised in the Pacific Northwest, he had fallen in love with art and storytelling at an early age, which ended up leading him to doing theater and writing in his free time growing up. You can find him on Instagram and Threads under the username @the_artur_faye, and read some of his other work on arturfaye.com